Alannah Hopkin

THE DOGS OF INISHERE

STORIES

DALKEY ARCHIVE PRESS

Library of Congress Cataloging-in-Publication Data

Names: Hopkin, Alannah, 1949-, author.
Title: The dogs of inishere : stories / Alannah Hopkin.
Description: First Dalkey Archive edition. | Victoria, TX : Dalkey Archive Press, 2017.
Identifiers: LCCN 2017003191 | ISBN 9781943150083 (pbk. : alk. paper)
Classification: LCC PR6058.O666 A6 2017 | DDC 823/.914--dc23
LC record available at https://lccn.loc.gov/2017003191

www.dalkeyarchive.com
Victoria, TX / McLean, IL / Dublin

Dalkey Archive Press publications are, in part, made possible through the support of the University of Houston-Victoria and its programs in creative writing, publishing, and translation.

Contents

The Dogs of Inishere

She was told in Rossaveale while she waited for the ferry that the islanders are great dog lovers. Nothing pleases them more than to be given a puppy to take home.

The ferry, the *Dun Aengus*, had a crew of two. It could have carried about forty passengers, but there were only a dozen or so on board and a clump of cardboard boxes. When they were close enough to the islands to distinguish between Inishmore, away the starboard beam, Inishmaan, the middle island, dead ahead, and Inishere the smaller island, just visible to port, the engine broke down.

The mate disappeared down a hatch. The captain joined him and without way they drifted, beam ends on to the Atlantic swell as diesel fumes swept up on deck and lingered there in spite of the breeze. A solemn-looking bearded man sitting opposite her stared anxiously back at the Connemara coast.

'I should have stayed with Delaney,' he said, looking straight at her. She pretended she hadn't heard.

Ten minutes later the captain re-emerged, sweaty forehead, greasy forearms, and gave a long exasperated explanation in Irish to a male passenger, concluding with the words 'fecking diesel'.

The captain pointed towards a house that did bed and breakfast as they landed at the pier. An old man sat in the garden twisting sally rods into small baskets. When he greeted another person after her she turned around to see that the bearded man who should have stayed with Delaney had followed her up.

'We made it,' he said. 'Is it your first time on the island?'

'Yes.'

'Inishere is different,' he said.

'So I've noticed. I can't get over all the gray stone. Gray stone and bleached-out grass, no colours at all. Even the sky is a paler blue.'

'Are you a painter?'

'I'm a photographer.'

A small English sheep dog type, gray and white and in need of grooming, lay on the doormat. He opened one milky eye, then grunted and turned over. Katy reached across and turned the latchkey, opening the door as Mrs. Flaherty came into the hall.

'Grand day.'

'The skipper on the ferry said you'd have rooms.'

'A double is it?'

'Two singles.'

'We're both from the ferry. The captain sent us over.'

'That would be Míhail, my nephew. He's very good to me.'

Mairead Flaherty stood in her front garden and pointed to a house with a wooden sign on its side: 'Restaurant'.

A small stone-walled field between the Flahertys house and the restaurant was occupied by an abandoned blue Ford Cortina. The field could have held two, at a pinch, it was that small. An under-nourished black and white bitch with something of a King Charles spaniel about her was sniffing around the rusting car. The field was a wildflower meadow. Harebells, scabious, purple clover, ox-eye daisies, saxifrage and bloody cranesbill grew among the tall grasses.

An L-shaped ground floor room had been furnished with simple tables and chairs. There were no curtains and the walls were plain apart from a framed certificate from the Western Health Board saying that the establishment was licensed as a 'limited restaurant'.

A shy young girl with a notepad came up to her.

The Dogs of Inishere

'Is the soup homemade?'

'No, it's from a packet.'

Only one other table was occupied. They were four women in their mid-twenties, drably turned out. The words 'chapel' and 'sister' occurred frequently in their conversation.

She walked from the restaurant back to the pier and on to the beach. It took about four minutes. The quiet was strange to her after the city. Cries from the bathers on the strand and the murmurs from people gossiping on the pier sounded eerie against the silence.

A short-legged terrier and a miniature mainly-Dachshund were hanging around on the pier. Neither they nor any of the other dogs on the island ever barked. She left them staring silently out to sea and walked barefoot onto the sand.

She watched as the Doolin ferry, a small motorboat with a very loud engine, made its way across to the pier. The four women from the restaurant were sitting in a cove with their backs to the rocks, each reading a paperback. As she stared towards the mainland, a speck appeared in the sky on the side of the island. A Land Rover suddenly roared up and down the landing strip scattering the donkeys that grazed there. The plane came in so low that she could watch the anxious faces of the passengers.

On her way back to the B&B, between the pier and the thatched cottage she met a medium-sized short-haired mongrel. One pat on the head made him lie at her feet grovelling in abject adoration, paws and nose stretched out on the ground. Then he rolled over and waved his legs in the air. He followed as she walked away, jumping up to lick her face, doggy breath warm on her cheeks, his long pink tongue hanging out of snapping, Alsatian-like jaws.

She changed from shorts into trousers, then went straight out again to the restaurant.

The man who should have stayed with Delaney was leaving it.

'Half an hour,' he said. 'They've forgotten to put the potatoes on. Michael Madden.'

She shook his hand.

'Katy Collins.'

'Shall we wait in the pub?'

'I haven't found it yet.'

'There are three, including the hotel. The nearest is Flaherty's.'

'Any relation to our B&B?'

'I don't know. We can ask.'

There was a line of young men along the bar and a low murmur of voices, which died down as they went in and then resumed. Everybody looked at them curiously and then looked away again.

She realised they had come in the back door that normally only locals used. A few tourists, easily identified by their smart casual clothes, were sitting at a table in the front window that looked out to the sea. She recognised a young couple and their small child who had got off the plane that afternoon. The bar had just been done up. There was a whiff of wood-shavings and glue. A space was made for Michael at the counter. A young man with curly black hair and bright blue eyes repeated his order: 'A gin and tonic and a glass of Guinness.' She took a seat on a wooden bench against the wall beside a small table.

'They're not related to the B&B, Piaras says, or not anymore,' Michael said as he sat down. 'They probably were long ago, Piaras says, but nowadays nearly everyone in this part of the island is called Flaherty. Do you have the melodious Gaelic on you?'

'Do you see me wearing a *fáinne*?'

'You must be from Kerry. Answering a question with a question.'

'What about you?'

'I had years of it at school, but it doesn't seem to have left any mark at all.'

'You've been to Inishere before?'

'Many times. But long ago. I've been living abroad. This is my first summer at home in years. I came up to Galway to stay with Delaney and I decided to take another look at the island.'

'And what do you reckon?'

'Well, this place has certainly changed. When I first knew it Piaras probably wasn't even born. I remember his father Tomás because he is the only publican ever to have refused me a drink. I wasn't drunk, not even noisy, I was just quietly sipping my gin and tonic up at the counter, and I asked for another. No, said Tomás Flaherty. You've had enough. And that was that. Another time I had to wait to be served while he finished the family rosary in the kitchen. He was in the wrong trade, they used to say. He should have been a bishop.'

She was trying to guess Michael's age as they watched a pale, elderly woman in dark glasses come up the front path. The woman stuck her head in the open door. She looked very worried:

'Has the last ferry left? They say the ferry went at four thirty but we were told on the way over that it was going back at six thirty.' She had a flat, unattractive American accent.

Piaras and his contemporaries up at the bar exchanged bored glances. One man said something in Irish and another answered him in an interrogative tone. Piaras was polishing a glass.

'Is there another ferry to Doolin today?' she was paler now, trembling slightly and biting her lip. 'Does anyone know if there's another Doolin ferry?'

They all looked at Piaras.

'I don't know the ferry times,' he said, still polishing the glass. 'Ask them below at the pier.'

That was obviously where she had just come from.

She turned and fled.

The young men up at the bar broke out laughing and the conversation became bi-lingual.

'Why does she expect me to know the fecking ferry times?'
said Piaras.

'It was the Rossaveale ferry left at half-four,' said another
young man, as if anyone who didn't know that must be very
stupid.

'The Doolin ferry goes at seven, doesn't it, Ruari?' said one
of the Irish speakers.

'It does not,' said a tall fat man. 'It goes at half-seven and I've
a ticket in my pocket.'

This remark caused great mirth among the locals.

The male of the well-dressed young couple at the window
joined in, speaking to the Doolin ferry ticket-holder:

'We're flying back to Galway tomorrow. We got a special
deal. A family ticket. The three of us fly for £38. The ferry
would have cost £12 each, there's not much in it.'

'We get subsidised fares. We can fly to Galway any time we
like, boy. Any time we like.'

The same couple sat next to Michael and Katy in the limited
restaurant. Katy liked Michael, who she decided was anything
from ten to twenty years older than her. He said he was an
engineer.

'If you're an engineer, why didn't you offer to help when the
boat broke down?'

'I'm not that sort of engineer. I build bridges.'

The name of the smart couple's child was Lauren.

'No, Lauren, you can't eat your Twix until you've had your
tea.'

'WANT IT NOW! WANT MY TWIX NOW!'

'You can't have your Twix until you've finished your steak.
Eat up now like a good girl.'

'WANT IT NOW!'

'Lauren!'

'WAAAA. WANNIT NOW!'

The wife smiled ingratiatingly at Katy across the table. Katy
looked away. The four young women were at the corner table

again. Lauren's roaring forced them to raise their voices, and again Katy caught the word 'sister' several times, and now 'theatre' as well.

She went for a walk with Michael afterwards, along narrow high-walled paths. An old-timer in a bawneen sweater passed them carrying a plastic bucket. He was on his way to milk the cow. Because the fields were so small there was only room for one cow in each. The cows looked sulky and bad-tempered.

'Cows are herd animals,' said Michael. 'They need company.'

About a mile from the restaurant they saw the child Lauren on her own, pushing an empty baby buggy up a path. From the distance she was invisible, hidden by the tall stone walls.

On their way back to the B&B they saw Lauren's young mother standing on a small hill, anxiously searching the horizon for her missing child.

At the front door they shook hands again. Michael asked if she would walk to the back of the island with him the next day.

'What's there?'

'Rocks. Sea. Wildflowers. It's different from this side of the island. No sandy beach. No houses.'

'No screaming kids?'

'Let's hope.'

'See you at breakfast.'

On Thursday afternoon Piaras Flaherty put the finishing touch to his redecoration: he installed a stereo radio and CD player. At six o'clock he went off to train for the currach races, leaving his brother behind the bar.

Two young men were leaning on it heavily, propping each other up. It was too much for the blond one: he slid to the floor and held on to the legs of a barstool. The dark-haired man kept trying to sing:

'Today I sold the old brown cow
For two pound ten . . .'

The brother behind the bar turned the radio on, full blast.

Heavy metal. Against which a voice was raised:
    'Today I sold the old brown cow
     For two pound ten . . .'
    'Dole day,' said Piaras's brother quietly as he handed Katy
and Michael their drinks.

'If you're a photographer, where are your cameras?' Michael
asked.
    'I'm on holiday.'
    They were eating in the hotel, sharing a bottle of red wine.
The waitress had put a candle on their table.
    'What shall we do tomorrow?' he asked.
    'We?'
    'You enjoyed today, didn't you?'
    'Yes.'
    'Then why not tomorrow?'
    'You're right. Why not?'

When Mairead served their breakfast next morning Michael
told her about yesterday in Flaherty's.
    'Dole day can get a bit out of hand alright, but we're glad to
have our people back. Unemployment has been a great help to
the island. If we have to choose between living on the dole in
Dublin or Galway, and living on the dole on the island, most of
us will choose the island. It's a great place to bring up children.'
    'And do the children stay?' Katy asked. 'Don't they want to
leave as soon as they can?'
    'The best way to know if the island is for you is to leave it.
I lived in Galway myself for long enough to get a degree in
Irish Studies and then I came back. Most of the people you see
here today have tried Galway or Dublin or Boston, and come
back. Often with children of their own. That's what keeps our
population steady.'
    When she was back in the kitchen they each quickly
buttered two slices of soda bread and put them in their pockets

for lunchtime on the back of the island. They had decided to move to Inishmaan that afternoon.

As they set off again for the back of the island they noticed that the dogs of Inishere had formed themselves into a pack. They were after the spaniel bitch. The sheep dog was followed by the groveller, his long pink tongue hanging from the side of his mouth, eyes straight ahead, fixed on the little bitch. Lagging behind, legs working as fast as they'd go, were the terrier and the little dachshund.

Later that day, as Michael and Katy were carrying their bags from the B&B to the pier they saw the terrier at the entrance to the Cortina field, stuck immobile to the spaniel. The sheep dog, the groveller and the dachshund were watching patiently, waiting their turn.

Ripe

Twelve noon Saturday, a muffled hum of traffic. Three hours since the pneumatic drill (gas board) dug up the road. Five hours since the council lorry removed the rubbish skip. Six hours since the metal-wheeled trolley delivered burgers to the fast food place. Nine hours since the dustmen. Nine hours in bed is enough.

Saturday. Launderette, Berwick Street market, supermarket, off-licence, flat cleaning, telly. Maybe work instead of telly? Maybe the flat's not dirty enough to clean? Maybe. Get up and see.

Awful hangover. Did I walk home alone last night? There does not appear to be anyone else in the bed. Just a book.

Malcolm Lowry: A Biography by Douglas Day.

Eh?

Bad.

Not remembering.

But not unusual lately.

Friday night at the French pub. Best night of the week. Best pub in Soho and that's not saying much. Hardly a pub at all.

Bath's scented steam clears the head—

'Still drunk and stumbling through the rusty trees
To breakfast on stale rum, sardines and peas'

Vaguely remember now. Arguing about Malcolm Lowry. I think I cried. Afterwards. When I got home.

Yes. It was Alfie, he was telling me a very beautiful story about going to Ripe on the twenty-fifth anniversary of Lowry's death, drinking gin and orange at the grave and leaving flowers in the empty gin bottle, then going into the church and writing that bit from 'Through the Panama' in the visitors' book:

'Gin and orange juice best cure for alcoholism, real cause of which is ugliness and complete baffling sterility of existence as sold to you.'

Then some old bore who'd been eavesdropping came lurching over and started to drone on about how Malcolm used to stay in his friend's flat in Battersea and they'd hide the gin in a gumboot under the kitchen sink and Malcolm always found it, what a great man for the drink, ho ho ho, you two should have known the French in Malcolm's day . . .

I thought he was going to go on about Dylan Thomas next, they usually do. That was when I decided to get even more drunk than usual and switched from white wine and soda to large glasses of claret. But I was wrong about Dylan Thomas. Soon everyone was talking about Malcolm Lowry, or so it seemed:

'Overrated. Only ever wrote on halfway good novel.'

'Complete mess. Absolute disaster area—'

'As for the verse . . .'

'No imagination, that was the trouble. All autobiographical—'

'No self-control either, totally self-indulgent—'

'His widow's still alive you know. Living in Los Angeles.'

'Poor Margerie, what she had to put up with—'

'Appalling place, Ripe, no wonder he kicked the bucket, living there.'

'Just a written out, middle-aged drunk—'

'Written out years before Ripe.'

It's not worth trying to argue with that crowd once they get going. Second-rate literary hangers-on who think they can impress anyone if they name-drop loudly enough.

I remember the first time I took Alfie to the French pub, it was half empty, but he said you could hardly find room to stand because of the size of the egos in there.

So, instead of arguing, I started to counterpoint their ramblings with Lowry quotes, and none of them even noticed what I was doing:

'The very sight of that old bastard makes me happy for five days. No bloody fooling.'

'Which one? The one near the door?'
'He reads and reads but does not understand.'
'Who?'
'No company but fear.'
'Didn't catch the name. Which company?'
'That arc of bar with its cracked brown paint.'
'Gaston doesn't dare redecorate. There'd be a riot.'
'The only hope is the next drink.'
'A large claret, was it, love?'

Alfie thought it was funny, but I got angry. All that they cared about was reciting second-hand Lowry anecdotes and airing their tired received opinions about his work. None of them had read *Under the Volcano* for years (if ever) and they'd obviously never opened a copy of the verse.

Fuck them, I kept thinking, as I got out of the bath and faced up to the Saturday chores.

The laundry basket was in a good state—nearly empty. The sheets would last another week, and the flat could get by with a five-minute sponge and duster job. That left food shopping.

I opened the windows a bit more and stuck my head out to check the weather. It was an average late August day—not sunny, but warm and dry. Clare from the flat above was crossing the road and we waved at each other.

As I turned back to the cheerful little one-room flat, I was shaken by the first surge of weekend depression. *Looming, the dreadful Pontefract of day* . . . I swore, and fought back, then closed my eyes for a few seconds.

For those few seconds I was lying in a field under a big blue sky listening to a lark.

I smiled ironically as I picked up my shopping bag and purse and headed off to Berwick Street.

Soho is different at weekends. Its population dwindles to a fraction of the weekday quota, and the only people you see around are locals and tourists. The tourists are not interested in the supermarket and the launderette, so the Saturday shopping round can be a very social time, you bump into all sorts of friends, and I'd often end up in The French or back at someone's flat for the afternoon.

I worked very hard doing PR for a film company in Old Compton Street, and went out almost every night during the week to all the latest films and plays and all kinds of restaurants. Everything was within walking distance of the flat, I earned enough money to enjoy it all, and I had a wide enough range of friends to avoid being alone unless I chose to be.

Most of my friends were living in the suburbs, and since I didn't have a car, only a bicycle (because of the parking problem) I found it easier to see them when they came up to the West End during the week, rather than trekking out to Acton, Stoke Newington, Wandsworth and the other newly gentrified areas where they had chosen to live.

They found my flat a convenient central meeting place, and enjoyed the novelty of knowing someone who actually *lived* in Soho. My friends tended to entertain at home at the weekends, and that suited me fine because I could keep Saturday and Sunday free to recover from Monday to Friday, organise myself for the next week and, in theory at least, work on my own writing.

The main disadvantage in that arrangement was that it would lead to attacks of a particular kind of urban claustrophobia. I could go for weeks on end without ever being more than half a mile away from Piccadilly Circus. It got to the point where a taxi ride to somewhere like Notting Hill became an occasion to savour and took on all the excitement of an annual school outing.

I had in fact been to Notting Hill by taxi before going to the French that Friday. I began to blame that trip for the unusually strong waves of weekend depression that hit me as I did the shopping. I kept remembering the leafy trees in the park beside the Bayswater Road, and how shocked I'd been to see that the horse-chestnut leaves were already turning, and summer would soon be over. Apart from that I hadn't noticed the summer much. When I rode the bicycle, I was too busy dodging the traffic to take in the scenery. Every time I used it, I seemed to have at least one near miss, so I was a very preoccupied cyclist. Summer meant wearing T-shirts and sandals, drinking in the street outside the French, and leaving the windows open at night.

I thought I had trained myself very efficiently not to think about what I was missing by living in Soho. I chose to live there because I hated commuting, and it seemed to make sense to find a place as central as possible. Being in the middle of all the action was supposed to compensate for such disadvantages as the constant noise and the smallness of the flat. But lately I'd found that I dreaded weekends. I never used to drink at weekends; there was quite enough of that during the week. Now I was drinking my way though the weekends as well to kill the boredom and numb my guilt at not writing.

By the time I got to Camisa's in Berwick Street, I decided that I needed a day out, a break from routine, a picnic even. I love picnics. I bought ham and Emmental and fresh rolls, and decided that on Sunday I would get up early, cycle to Holland Park with a novel and a notebook and lie on the grass looking up at the sky. You don't see much sky in Soho, just small patches between buildings.

Back at the flat I unpacked the shopping and, because my head had cleared up, I opened a bottle of Chablis that I found in the fridge. Someone must have left it there the week before. I sat back in the armchair sipping, and picked up the Lowry biography again, opening it at Chapter One:

'The village of Ripe is in East Sussex, about five miles due east of the town of Lewes, just north of the South Downs.'

Suddenly the bleak weekend ahead of me had a point. I would make the pilgrimage to Ripe, the Lowry trek. It was such a simple and obvious idea, but it was enough to lift the depression and replace it with a mildly manic euphoria.

At first I thought of asking a friend with a car to come with me, but I couldn't think of anyone suitable, especially not at such short notice. I thought about hiring a car, but the prospect of Sunday traffic on the Brighton road, and the implication of little or no drinking put me off that idea.

Instead, I decided to take the bicycle on the train to Lewes, and cycle from Lewes to Ripe. I phoned Victoria Station for Sunday morning train times, then I walked up to Foyles and bought a good map with the relevant part of Sussex on it.

Ripe was in the middle of a triangle with Lewes, Polegate and Glyndebourne at each corner. Glyndebourne came as a surprise. I'd never been there either.

I spent the rest of the afternoon in a state of childish excitement, checking the bicycle, studying the map—there seemed to be at least three different ways of getting from Lewes to Ripe—searching for my lightweight anorak and deciding what else to take with me.

I settled for the City Lights edition of Lowry's verse, my camera and a new notebook.

I decided to give myself a complete break from the half-written novel that I was supposed to be working on during these empty Soho weekends. After a heavy week doing public relations for feature films, it's very hard to switch back to one's own work. There are really no excuses: it's just difficult. I can't blame interruptions: I'd leave my phone on the answering machine and ignore the doorbell. But first there were chores, which mounted up alarmingly if I left them. And I was always tired on Saturdays, so it was tempting to collapse in front of the television. I seldom had a chance to watch it during the week.

On Sundays I'd get up very late, read the papers, and by the time I sat down at the table to 'work' it would be about five o'clock. Knowing that I only had a few hours ahead of me, I was reluctant to immerse myself too deeply in the project, and spent most of the time looking out of the window at tourists going in and out of the sex shop opposite, cars parking, people arguing,

kids sniffing glue, winos falling over . . . the old street drama is
very distracting in Soho.

In spite of, or perhaps because of my decision not to worry
about the novel, that was the first Saturday for many months
on which I managed to get down to work by early evening. I
started to feel as if, for once, my apparently well-organised life
really was well-organised.

I didn't do so well on Sunday morning. I overslept, probably
because of that second bottle of wine. I missed the 10.20 train
and somehow I also missed the 11.20. That meant getting
the 12.20. I probably wouldn't make it to Ripe in time for a
lunchtime pint at Lowry's local as planned. But, according to
the biography, the Lowrys had been banned from The Lamb,
Ripe's only pub, because Margerie had sworn at the landlady
for selling Malcolm a bottle of gin. They walked to The Yew
Tree in Chalvington, a mile away, on the few occasions when
they went out for a drink. So it didn't matter much, missing The
Lamb.

One thing that I have in common with Malcolm Lowry is
a dislike of being a tourist in any circumstances, and an extra
special self-consciousness about being a literary tourist with
notebook and camera. You might remember that story he wrote
about a visit to Keats's house in Rome—'Strange Comfort
Afforded by the Profession'. That was why I had never been to
Ripe before.

So it was with the greatest suspicion that I observed two
other people getting off the train at Lewes with bicycles. A man
and a woman, about my age, and they had all the right touring
equipment, unlike me. My bicycle seldom travelled further
than Chelsea or Chalk Farm, so I had no need for ten gears,
drop handlebars, rucksacks, panniers, and toe straps. And had
I wanted one, that kind of bike wouldn't last a week in Soho,
even double-chained to the railings with the sex shop touts
across the road keeping an eye on it, which was how mine spent
most of its time.

It is, I'll have to admit, an academic-looking bicycle, scruffy, black and solid, with a well-worn basket on the front, three gears, a dynamo and old-fashioned straight handlebars. It would blend in well in Cambridge. On the platform at Lewes it seemed to scream out 'I belong to a literary lady on a pilgrimage to Ripe'. But, in the unlikely event that those other cyclists were doing the same thing, they'd be there and back before I arrived.

I knew from the map that I had to turn right out of the station. I hadn't known what a steep hill it would be, and before I was half-way up, I had to get off and push. I was not fit at all. Then there was a busy bit of main road, a roundabout, the outskirts of Lewes, and finally I came to the first turning off the main road.

It curved along between high hedges for about half a mile and I began to relax and congratulate myself on having had such a good idea, and on being organised enough to see it through. I relaxed so much that I took my eyes off the road in front of me, stopped worrying about traffic (there wasn't any) and looked around.

The road was sloping down, the hedges were lower now and on either side of me were small grassy fields and barns and little lanes under an overcast sky. Ahead, the road I was travelling curved up and away to the right, and as I pedalled along I could watch a field dotted with black and white cows change shape as the perspective created by the hedges moved in relation to my position.

I was stunned by the beauty of it. It must have been years since I'd ridden a bicycle in the country, and I'd forgotten that cycling could be fun. It was something very simple, but very strong, a feeling of exaltation and awe similar to the one that Lowry caught at the end of that sonnet called 'Happiness':

A new kind of tobacco at eleven,
And my love returning on the four o'clock bus
– My God, why have you given this to us?

The church is just outside Ripe. I found it easily, then I spent half an hour searching for the grave. I remembered that the biography had said it was at the edge of the consecrated ground, small, usually untended and inscribed:

Malcolm Lowry

1909 – 1957

I hadn't expected it to be quite so small. A plain, gray headstone, barely a foot tall, the simplest and therefore the saddest grave you could imagine. Only forty-eight years on this earth. Such a short life, so much unwritten. I knelt, suddenly unselfconscious and able to trust my own instincts about the right thing to do.

Then I leant against a stone wall opposite the grave to eat my lunch.

After lunch I sat on the grave for a couple of hours. Malcolm Lowry's presence was very strong. I suppose that's why people do this sort of thing, but I never believed it would happen to me. It was as if he were alive and cross-examining me impatiently about my life and my work. I learnt a lot in those quiet moments with Malc.

No Rupert Brooke and no great lover, he
remembered little of simplicity.

So he described himself in a poem called 'He Liked the Dead'. Great title.

He's the only hero I've ever had. I don't like having heroes. I first read *Under the Volcano* when I was fourteen, and have re-read it about once a year ever since. That, the stories and the verse, the unfinished works and the letters have fed my obsession with writing far more effectively than the greats like Joyce and Beckett. I'm not sure why.

In the end there are very few people living or dead who have a positive effect on one's life. It seemed some homage and thanks were due.

I sat on the grave with the notebook, not writing, just staring at the headstone. He seemed to enjoy the company. It was okay because I'd already paid him homage in the only way he would have cared about: by reading and (up to a point) understanding his work, his hell. And being there, with Malcolm Lowry, I was able to think clearly about my work and (as I came to realise) my hell, for the first time in years.

Later I walked back up to Ripe and found some purple wild flowers in a ditch on the other side of the village. I picked armfuls, and went back to the grave without looking for his rented house. Pointless to stand and stare at that.

I borrowed an urn from another grave, put the flowers in the urn and stood it on Malcolm's grave. Then I took pictures of the grave from all angles. The two best ones are pinned up on the wall in front of me as I write.

I left Ripe in a daze, intending to return to Lewes by another road that went through Glyndebourne. I got lost and ended up in Polegate. The railway station was signposted, and ten minutes short of Sunday opening time I was sitting, blatantly thirsty, outside the Station Arms. There was a train at seven, another at eight, and a third at nine. A Lowry trek without a drink is unthinkable.

I drank beer until five to nine. There were only a few locals in the small bar, and they showed no interest in me. I had hoped they would ask where I'd been so that I could reply, 'I was visiting a friend in Ripe'. As it was, they left me alone to think.

The decision had been made in Ripe. Seeing Soho again only confirmed it. I double-chained the bike to the railing, waved at Larry who was on duty at the sex shop, let myself into the flat and made a big pot of coffee. Then I pulled the curtains on the street scene, the cruising drunks and the flickering neon, and wrote a letter to some friends who were living almost self-sufficiently in Wales.

I had to go somewhere rural, quiet and cheap. Wales was as good as anywhere. I'd spent a weekend in west Wales with

Paul and Sally a few years before, and they had mentioned how cheap it was to rent places there. I liked the area, and their friends, not all of whom were dedicated to self-sufficiency. It would be a start.

Then I made a list of saleable assets, the major one being the fixtures and fittings on the flat. Key money in effect, because I wasn't planning to leave anything in it. Two people had already asked for first option if I ever moved, and I reckoned I would get three or four times more than I'd paid for fixtures and fittings myself, which would give me more than enough cash to live on quietly for eighteen months or more.

The dustmen came and went at one o'clock. By the time they delivered burgers on the meal-wheeled trolley, I'd typed a letter of resignation to the film company and was completely absorbed in re-reading *Under the Volcano*. I fell asleep as the council lorry arrived to pick up the rubbish skip and didn't surface until the traffic snarled up at ten o'clock and woke me by hooting. I walked to work as usual and delivered the letter to the managing director.

New Girl

DEIRDRE O'CONNELL WAS a quiet, serious girl who loved reading, horses and her cat, Naseby. Naseby was a black cat with green eyes, almost totally silent. She and Deirdre were devoted to each other: Deirdre talked to Naseby, and Naseby hissed at strangers if they got too close to Deirdre. Occasionally, for no apparent reason, Naseby would give one long, heart-rending cry, then look around with narrowed green eyes to see if anyone had noticed. 'Naseby has a sense of humour,' was Deirdre's explanation.

She had friends at her day school, St. Anselm's, in the south London suburbs, but seldom saw them outside school hours. She preferred to read, or talk to Naseby, or add to the list of new words that she kept in a notebook called <u>Vocabulary</u>. Her brother Daniel had just got his first car, and he organised a series of days out on the summer weekends: Knole, Hever Castle, Penshurst Place. Daniel was interested in history and architecture, and assumed Deirdre shared his interests, which he explained to her at some length. One Friday night, on his way to read her the ritual bedtime story, he overheard her telling Naseby: 'Daniel's got another outing planned tomorrow, Naze. Igtham Mote. Did you ever hear such an idiotic name? Will you go *nowhere* with me on Sunday?'

This was her last term at Saint Anselm's, and in the autumn most of her friends were going on to the local convent, a longer bus ride away. But Deirdre's mother wanted Deirdre to board at St Teresa's, a smaller school in the Surrey countryside, which had been attended by Deirdre's Irish cousins ten years before. If it was good enough for them, said Mrs O'Connell, then it was good enough for Deirdre.

Her mother thought that Deirdre spent too much time alone, reading, or talking to her cat. At boarding school her mother believed that Deirdre would make suitable friends from a similar background, who spoke nicely, without the cockney accent that lurked in their suburb. At boarding school she would learn to be more sociable and start to behave like a normal child. St Teresa's had its own riding stables and Deirdre would have the run of the Surrey countryside for ten guineas a term extra, instead of just a one-hour hack on Wimbledon Common every Saturday morning. Daniel was off to college to study architecture, so, thought Mrs. O'Connell, with Daniel away, and Deirdre at boarding school, there would be no need for a temperamental au pair in the spare room; an obliging neighbor could feed Naseby, and she and her husband would be free to travel.

Shopping for school uniforms confirmed Deirdre's suspicions that boarding school was going to be totally unlike anything she had read about in Enid Blyton or the girls' comics that her school friends liked. Her mother took her to a special shop off Oxford Street that sold nothing but school uniforms. She liked the games kit, especially the hockey boots and the green and yellow striped socks, but she could not disguise her dislike of the Harris Tweed suit. Her friends from St Anselm's would be wearing dark blue gymslips at their new school. Why did St Teresa's have to be different? The tweed was like cardboard. The skirt had a deep pleat front and back, and a short boxy jacket with three large buttons that reminded her of Oughterard, a place she disliked intensely. She and Daniel always wrote 'Ookter-ard'. Her Irish cousins lived near Oughterard, where her mother was from originally. It was the sort of suit a bossy old woman in Oughterard would wear to Mass. Worst of all was the colour, an unpleasant shade of green described in the clothing list as 'moss green', which also reminded her of Oughterard, where moss grew everywhere.

Her mother continued to cross items off the list, under the eagle eye of an elderly shop assistant: 'Twelve pairs of sixty denier stockings, dark tan. Does she really need twelve pairs?'

'Can't I wear knee socks, mummy? I hate stockings for everyday, and these aren't even proper nylons. Only old ladies wear sixty denier.'

'You're a big girl now, Deirdre. No more kneesocks. Except for games: hockey socks, two pairs, netball socks, two pairs, one dark green divided skirt, two white Aertex shirts . . . I don't see why you can't play netball in your hockey socks, but we have to go by the list.'

Afterwards they went to Lyons Corner House at Marble Arch. Deirdre had hot chocolate and hot-buttered toast while Mrs. O'Connell drank a pot of tea and tried to forget the enormous bill that she had just run up.

Deirdre stood alone outside the Gym beside her weekend case feeling very lost and lonely, a stray in the rain, and waved at the back of her father's car, SUF 80. The stately motor car's warm interior with its familiar smell of leather, was gone, gobbled up by the tunnel of trees as it went down the hilly entrance drive, until its familiar back number plate disappeared completely. She hoped her parents had not seen the tears streaming down her face, and wiped them away with the back of her hand. But more kept coming and her nose was running, and she could not find a handkerchief even though she had six of them somewhere each marked with an embroidered nametape saying Deirdre O'Connell 52. She'd helped her mother finish the marking only the night before. Every piece of clothing had to have a nametape, and her mother had celebrated with a large whiskey and soda when the very last one was sewn on.

The memory of that moment made her realise why she was crying, and where this blind panic came from. In spite of being almost five foot tall, she felt very small. There was a voice inside her head repeating loudly: 'I want to go home. Now! There's been a terrible mistake!'

But she knew there was no escape. She took a big sniff, scowled and wiped her nose on the back of her hand, reminding herself that she was not a baby. She was twelve years old. Just. She had no idea where to go or what to do next, and the drizzle was getting heavier. Suddenly a large black shape loomed out of the mist, waddling towards her under a black umbrella. Mother Joanna.

'Deirdre! Here is Kathleen. She is the head of your table in the Refectory, and she is going to help you to settle in.'

A bigger girl appeared and picked up Deirdre's weekend bag. 'Welcome to St Teresa's. I'm Kathleen, and I'm going to help you to unpack.' She handed Deirdre a handkerchief. 'Don't worry, it happens to most of us in the first term. Gets a bit better in the second term, but there's even girls in my year who howl their eyes out every time they come back. Even in the Upper Fourth, imagine that!'

Deirdre did not know what the Upper Fourth was, but she tried to look impressed as she followed Kathleen into the huge open space of the Gym.

'You're in Green Dorm. Some of the first years like Green better than Pink because there's only twelve of you. There's twenty-four in Pink, so you get some second years as well. Nicer to be just first years, isn't it?'

They located Deirdre's trunk, and each picked up an armful of clothes. Kathleen led the way through a door beside the stage and up a short flight of stairs that led to a narrow corridor. Green Dorm was a long dark room. There was nothing green about it except its name. Deirdre knew at once that there would be no midnight feasts in this dormitory.

'Good afternoon, Mother Francis,' said Kathleen in a singsong voice.

'Good afternoon, Kathleen. Welcome back.'

'Thank you, Mother. This is Deirdre O'Connell.'

'Welcome to St Teresa's, Deirdre.'

'Thank you, Mother.' Her voice came out tiny and tearful.

Ten of the narrow beds in Green Dorm were lined up with their heads to the wall, as dormitory beds should be. Two more had been squeezed in parallel to the opposite wall, forming a corridor between the feet of the other beds. Deirdre was given one of the beds on the corridor parallel to the wall. She thought it was the worst bed in the dorm.

Kathleen was head of Deirdre's table in the junior dining room. Supper consisted of tea, sliced white bread and marmalade. Deirdre thought it was strange to have marmalade on the supper table and quietly ate one slice of bread and funny-tasting butter.

'Here we go again, cut loaf and marge and stewy tea,' said the girl next to her. 'You're new, aren't you?'

'Yes. Why have they given us marmalade for supper? At home we only have marmalade for breakfast.'

'Don't worry. You'll soon get the hang of it. My name's Melody.'

She was about the same age as Deirdre, but she seemed totally at ease, and she hadn't been crying.

'I'm Deirdre. Are you new too?'

'Sort of, but not really. I was at Grove House, that's the junior school. But it's my first term in the big school.'

'Tea, Deirdre.' Kathleen was at her elbow with a cup of metallic-smelling dark orange liquid.

'No thank you, I don't drink tea,' said Deirdre.

'You don't drink tea?' Kathleen seemed to think it was very funny. 'Hey, Sue, I've got one that doesn't drink tea!' She was talking to the big girl at the head of the next table, and pointing at Deirdre. Deirdre stared at her plate and hated big girls and people who drank tea with all her heart.

Vocabulary

Ref: short for refectory, where you eat your meals.

Supervision: when there is always a nun in the room, usually the Gym at weekends or a classroom for Prep. Obligatory for under-thirteens.

Prep: when you do your homework in a classroom, under Supervision, in silence.

Lukewarm: temperature of water in the urn from which you fill your hot water bottle in the dorm. Also temperature of the radiators in the Gym, and the water in the hot tap, hence of the water in your bath, which you can only have twice a week at 4.30pm on Tuesdays and Thursdays. Lukewarm.

Hottie: short for hot water bottle. Only idiots say hottie.

Chilblain: painful thing you get on your hands from hanging on to the radiator in Supervision. Can also be got on your feet.

Verruca: different kind of painful thing you get on your feet from walking barefoot on dirty floors.

Clay: something that makes the mud around here extra-sticky.

Bronco: toilet paper that leaves your fingers smelling of disinfectant.

Horsehair mattress: thin thing you sleep on that has to be stripped every morning and turned over to get the lumps out and be aired.

Mascot: what girls my age call their teddy bears. Idiots.

Cut loaf: stuff we get instead of bread.

Marge: stuff we spread on cut loaf instead of butter.

Mufti: what you wear when you are not in uniform; only permitted on special occasions.

Conduct mark: what you are given for breaking a rule. Three conduct marks make a penalty, but sometimes you do something so serious that you are given a penalty straight off. There are four Houses in competition and if you get a penalty you let down your House. Five penalties mean you are off-privileges.

Privileges: Riding is a privilege even though we pay extra for it, and so is tuck, and so are visiting weekends and wearing mufti on Sunday afternoons.

Day girls: One hundred and twenty girls who arrive on coaches every morning from Monday to Friday and go home every evening, where they have central heating, fitted carpets, sofas, televisions, hot chocolate, brothers, pets and other things that us boarders have to do without.

'I've got three brothers and they're all at Downside,' said Melody Tarrant, as they ran around the perimeter of the hockey pitch on Saturday morning a week later. Her tone of voice was challenging Deirdre to come up with something as good.

'My brother was at Douai. He was captain of the hockey team. And the cricket team.'

Melody was impressed. 'I'll ask mine if they know him. They play Douai all the time. What's his name?'

'Daniel. But he's left now.'

'Gosh. He must be awfully much older than you.'

'Eight years. He had a hockey trial for Surrey.'

'No wonder you're so good. I'm sure you'll be on the team next term.' Melody was the youngest player on the junior team, and very proud of it.

'I don't think I'm coming back next term.'

''Course you are! After all that money your parents spent on the uniform? Especially the Harris Tweed suit. You don't think they'll let you get away with just one term, do you? Anyway, you have to give a term's notice or else the nuns make you pay the fees.'

'My parents wouldn't mind.'

'Are they very rich?'

'I don't think so. Daddy's a doctor.'

'Oh, so's mine! Isn't that funny? Come on, let's run faster this time round.'

Deirdre trotted round the pitch behind Melody. By the third circuit she stopped wanting to cry and resigned herself to the idea of two terms at St Teresa's. Running around the hockey pitch was the only way she knew of to escape Supervision. Mother Joanna could keep an eye on them from the Gym windows.

Deirdre liked to run as fast as she could until she was almost out of breath, and then, just when she thought she'd have to stop, she would catch her second wind and go on and on pounding through the crisp autumn air. While the other under-thirteens huddled around the lukewarm radiators with their knitting, or played halfhearted games of Grandmother's Footsteps, Melody and Deirdre ran up and down the hockey pitch seeing who could dribble a ball fastest, taking turns to tackle each other or practise bullying-off or, as now, simply running around the perimeter of the pitch. Round and round and round.

After the fresh air the cloakroom always seemed stuffy and cheesy. Deirdre hated having to change out of games kit and put on her Harris Tweed skirt and fasten her stockings on to her suspender belt, which pinched her waist, and knot her tie under the collar of her beige wool sweater, which prickled her skin.

Melody and Deirdre were in different houses, which was a disappointment to Deirdre. She looked enviously at Melody's tie which was striped green and yellow all the way down as she tied her own which had only one yellow stripe on it.

'I wish I was in St Luke's House with you,' said Deirdre. 'I'm dreading the House Meeting.'

'Why? You haven't got any penalties, have you?'

'No. But I haven't got any merits either.'

'No one will mind, you're only a new girl.' Melody had finished changing and stood up to check the straightness of her stocking seams.

'Buck up! We'd better get back to Supervision or we might get a conduct mark.'

Deirdre sat on a bench in her alphabetically allocated place. Each new girl had to stand up and be welcomed by Mother Conception, St John's House Mistress. The girl on Deirdre's left was tall and thin with long straight blonde hair tied in a ponytail. Deirdre noticed that she already had bosoms. She was probably wearing a bra. Mother Conception called out 'Sara

Oates', and Deirdre's neighbour stood up as Mother Conception continued: '69, Upper Three "C". Pink Dormitory.' Sara Oates sat down again, landing heavily on the bench next to Deirdre. Now it was her turn. Her knees were shaking. It only took seconds: her name, her number, her form—Upper Three "A"—and her dormitory were read out, and she sat down again with a slight thump, just as Sara had done. Sara bounced up from the bench and giggled a little as she landed. Deirdre bounced back and smiled at her and almost laughed. Mother Conception continued her list of new girls: 'Sonia Orlov. 121. Upper Three "A". Pink Dormitory.'

Sonia looked too big to be in Upper Three, and Deirdre could not remember having seen her in class. She would not have forgotten that heavy straight black hair and the perfectly straight nose. Mother Conception was still talking: 'Sonia has joined us late in the term due to . . . er . . . unforeseen circumstances. I would ask you all to be especially kind to Sonia and to make sure that she knows her way around. Stand up again, Sonia, so that everyone can have a good look at you.'

Sonia stood up straight, looking down on the upturned faces around her, and slowly turned a full circle before sitting down gently on the bench, without the slightest thump. Deirdre's open-mouthed admiration at this display of elegance and composure was disturbed by a dig in the ribs. Sara Oates was miming applause by silently clapping her hands beside her knee. Deirdre had bumped into Sonia after the nudge, and Sonia saw the applause. She made a gesture in Sara's direction also at knee level with one upraised middle finger, and Sara made an explosive noise in her nose and covered her face with her hands as if she were stifling a sneeze, while she shook with laughter. Deirdre ignored this bad behaviour and turned her attention back to Mother Conception's speech: '. . . more than five penalties and privileges are lost. Penalties must be paid for either by washing up or detention, and this is in addition to the loss of privileges. Privileges are as follows . . .'

Next to the food, Supervision was Deirdre's biggest hate. The games of tag and I-Spy and Grandmother's Footsteps in the Gym were babyish and pointless. From the very start she made it clear that she preferred to read, and eventually she was left alone, and not asked to take part. She disliked being constantly in the presence of other people, constantly expected to interact with others, be polite about their knitting or crochet. She disliked having to sit up all day: at home she liked to lie on the warm wool carpet while reading a book, or sideways across an armchair, or with her feet up on a sofa. Here there were only bare boards on the draughty floor, and no armchairs at all. She often wished she could disappear on her own with a good book, like the rainy afternoons she spent on her bedroom floor with Naseby asleep beside her.

She had read *Black Beauty*, the only horsey book in the book cupboard that passed for a school library, and did not want to read it again because it made her cry. None of the other well-worn books in the cupboard, which were mainly religious, interested her. Mother Joanna gave her *The Mill on the Floss*, a fat book with small print in a tattered leather cover. There were obviously not going to be any horses in it, and Deirdre strongly suspected there would not be a happy ending either. But she carried the book around with her anyway, so that she could pretend to be reading, and have an excuse for not joining in the games.

She was walking in single file from the Ref to Green Dorm one evening after tea, when she was startled by a white-faced nun, who suddenly darted out from a dark corner at the top of the stairs.

'Devious,' the nun hissed. 'That's what you are, Deirdre O'Connell, you're deviousssss.'

She didn't know where to look or what to say, so she looked at the floor.

'Devious,' the nun repeated, and pushed her back into the line of girls so roughly that she bumped into Sara Oates and nearly knocked her over. Only then did she realise it was Mother Francis, the nun in charge of her dorm. Her face had been so distorted by hatred that she had not recognised her. She heard a familiar throaty laugh behind her, and saw Sara Oates exchange looks with Sonia Orlov. Sara made a thumbs-up sign, which Deirdre pretended not to have seen.

The next day during Supervision Deirdre went into a corner with the dictionary and looked up devious: *deceitful; tortuous of mind; winding; roundabout; out of the way; remote; erring. Adv. Deviously, n. deviousness. See deviate.*

The word devious came between devil and devise.

One dark Saturday afternoon, as Deirdre was going from the Gym to the Green Dorm to change her stocking, which was laddered, she noticed for the first time a cupboard on her right, a small wooden cupboard with a door from floor to ceiling with three air holes about an inch wide drilled into it. On the wall opposite the cupboard was a tall sash window that looked out on to the setting sun. Deirdre tried the handle of the door, and found it was a simple lifting mechanism, unlocked. Inside was a low-ceilinged space, occupied by a folded carpet. It smelt faintly of incense and dust. When she closed the door, sunlight streamed in through the air holes. The folded carpet made a natural armchair. She sat down and stretched out her legs and listened to the perfect silence, while dust motes danced in the sun's last rays. It was heaven: a small, private place. All she needed was a good book.

Sara Oates sat down with her usual bounce on the Gym bench next to Deirdre and peered over her shoulder.

'You're not really reading that book, are you?' she said quietly. 'I've been watching you. You're just pretending. Good idea. Anything's better than Granny's bloody Footsteps. Whoops! I didn't shock you, did I?'

'Course not. I've got a brother who says bloody all the time.'

'So have I! He's at the Oratory. And my father thinks it's funny when I swear, so I do it a lot at home. He encourages me, mainly to annoy my mother, she says.'

'You're not usually in Supervision, are you?'

'I should be. But I have to do an awful lot of piano practice.' Sara nodded solemnly. 'Hours and hours of piano practice. I practise the piano every day.'

'Lucky you. Maybe I should take up music instead of riding. The riding is a swiz.'

'I know. I did riding last year when I was in Grove House. One measly hour a week, and not allowed to muck out or tack up until you're thirteen. Music is much better value, if you know what I mean. Today I have to do extra practice, and I don't have a page-turner. Sonia's in the infirmary.'

'Oh, I'm sorry.'

'Nothing wrong with her, she just fancied a rest, a day in bed with Horlicks and a hot water bottle. She can twist matron round her little finger.'

Deirdre's face gave nothing away, but she felt a lightness of spirit creeping over her, and the unfamiliar sensation of a smile forming on her face.

'I could turn the pages for you if you like. I've done years and years of piano, but I gave up when I passed Grade Three.'

'If you could possibly drag yourself out of that book . . .'

'Let's go and ask Mother Joanna.'

The hour between teatime and Prep on weekdays was the easiest time to escape Supervision, as the supervising nun never checked the excuses offered for being absent from the Gym: extra maths, hockey practice, piano practice or the organised walk in pairs to the back gate lodge. Deirdre, Sara and Sonia always gave individual excuses, then met up in front of the school, and disappeared into an ancient rhododendron bush so large that it had paths meandering through it. In summer it was a popular place to sit and gossip without the risk of being overheard by a nun, but it was too cold to linger in winter. On the far side of the rhododendron bush was an unfrequented path that led to an area where the gardening nuns left large piles of leaves to rot in heaps contained by wire mesh. All the leaves had been swept up, and the path was unfrequented. Beyond the leaf pile, the path dwindled, and ended at a disused back gate on to a public road, which the girls squeezed through. 'Out of bounds! Out of bounds!' they shouted, jumping up and down on the tarmac to get warm. It was currently their favourite game, accumulating imaginary penalties. Then they squeezed back in, and out again, several times. 'Six penalties!' said Sonia, 'If anyone saw us. In and out six times! Each. One penalty for each out-of-bounds. Six penalties each!'

'And another for not being in Supervision!' said Deirdre. 'Seven penalties!' Then they ran back up the hill in the dusk, past the leaf pile, through the rhododendron bush and in the back door near the kitchen, and up the corridor that passed the empty Ref and led to the Gym. The door to the Ref was open, and a bowl of apples sat on the sideboard. Sonia darted in, picked up an apple, threw it up in the air and shouted 'Geronimo!' All three watched in horror as the apple spun towards the high sash window and smashed through the glass.

'Run,' they spoke as one, and disappeared around the corner, stopping for a moment outside the Gym to catch their breath.

'Why on earth did you do that?' asked Sara.

'I've no idea,' said Sonia. 'It just happened.'

'It flew through the window!' said Deirdre. 'Free at last! It was beautiful. Beautiful.'

School lessons at St Teresa's were either deadly dull or idiotic, in Deirdre's opinion, dull being the things she could understand—English, history, geography, biology—and idiotic the things she could not make any sense of—French, Latin, maths. So far

English had consisted of *The Lady of Shalott* being read aloud in class and the teacher droning on about it. Then one day shortly before half term, copies of this year's set book were given out: *Jane Eyre* by Charlotte Bronte. The plan was to read one chapter aloud in each English lesson, and then discuss it. 'There was no possibility of taking a walk that day.' From the opening sentence Deirdre was hooked. Everyone else put their books away in their desks at the end of the class. Deirdre carried hers with her to Supervision, and went on reading.

'Look at her!' said Melody Tarrant on her way to hockey practice. 'She's reading the English set book! Did you ever see anything more stupid? Goody-goody!'

But Deirdre was lost to the world. Here at last was a heroine she understood, a heroine lacking 'a sociable and childlike disposition', treated unfairly by the world. It was as if the book had been written only for her: 'I was conscious that a moment's mutiny had already rendered me liable to strange penalties, and, like any other rebel slave, I felt resolved, in my desperation, to go to all lengths.'

Mother Joanna came and sat beside her, and took out her knitting. 'You have a new book, Deirdre. Show me.'

'*Jane Eyre*, Mother Joanna. It's our English set text, but I want to know what happens next.'

'I believe Mother Benignus is leading a walk to the back gate lodge. You would be better off getting some fresh air while it is not raining.'

'Please, Mother Joanna, I'd rather read my book.'

'Off you go now, and put on your wellingtons. Plenty of time for reading in school hours and Prep.'

On her way to the cloakroom, Deirdre remembered that the socks she wore under her wellingtons were up in Green Dorm, having just come back from the wash. She was still carrying *Jane Eyre* as she passed the strange little cupboard full of carpet on her way from the Gym to the Dorm. She had just read about Jane hiding herself behind a curtain on the window seat to study

Bewick's *History of British Birds*, and a brainwave struck her. Mother Joanna thought she had gone on Mother Benignus's walk, but Mother Benignus wasn't expecting her. She could escape for what was left of the hour before Prep by hiding in the cupboard with her book. A warm glow of anticipation spread through her: it was a perfect plan. She looked both ways, just in case, and opened the cupboard door. Outside was a light switch, belonging to a single light bulb hanging from the ceiling. She clicked it on, lay back on the carpet and resumed her reading of Chapter Two. The coincidence of what she read gave her a pleasant shiver of recognition: 'This room was chill because it seldom had a fire; it was silent because remote from the nursery and kitchen; solemn because it was known to be so seldom entered.'

'Five penalties! All at once! Five real penalties! Tell us again about Mother Francis!'

'She was on her way up to Green Dorm, and she saw the light, so she tore the door open and put her horrible head right in to the cupboard, and she roared at me, she really roared: Deirdre O'Connell! Lying on the Holy Chapel Carpet! Come out of there immediately, you bad, bad girl. I always knew you were devious, but this is the limit! Then she marched me off to Reverend Mother's study, and I had the whole thing again, the Holy Chapel Carpet, the carpet that is laid on the Sanctuary while the Blessed Sacrament is exposed, bad behaviour, very bad behaviour, the worst they had come across so far this term, and five penalties.'

'That's a record for a new girl,' said Sara. 'Well done.'

'And good timing,' said Sonia. 'It's half term next week. If it was just a visiting weekend, they could keep you in school because you're off privileges, but half term isn't a privilege, it's obligatory, so they can't stop you going home. You'll have four whole days away from this dump, just concentrate on that, and don't let detention and the washing up get you down.'

'I can't wait to tell my father,' said Sara. 'He's going to love this story: Mother Francis and the Holy Chapel Carpet! It's bloody marvellous, that's what he'll say, bloody marvellous!'

Home at last. Daniel was home from Bristol too, for the first two days of her half term. Snuggled down in her warm, well-sprung bed, chintz curtains drawn against the orange street light, lying on her side, with Naseby curled up between her knees, her hand stroking the purring cat on the back of the neck, she was close to heaven. The reading light was still on, but *Jane Eyre* was face down on the carpet, and the door ajar.

Daniel crept up to the door, wondering whether Deirdre had already fallen asleep, but no, she was talking to Naseby. He hesitated, reluctant to interrupt the calm, confiding tone of voice.

'So you see, Naze, I tried awfully hard to be good, but it was horrible, all the time. Then this nun, Mother Francis, told me I was devious, *devioussss*, and that made Sara and Sonia laugh, and quite by accident, I started behaving badly. I didn't mean to, it just happened and it was so much more fun. You'd really like Sara and Sonia, they're bad too, but they don't get caught. I got caught, and I got five penalties, more than any other new girl, and now everyone wants to be my friend. Except Melody Tarrant. So school's not as bad as I thought it was at first, just different. But I don't think I'll be there for much longer . . .'

She sighed, and seemed to fall asleep. Daniel started to tiptoe away, but a floorboard creaked, and he heard the familiar peremptory call: 'Please can I have a glass of water? Not kitchen water, bathroom water? And a story?'

Twentyquidsworth

'YOU KNEW DAN O'NEILL, didn't you?'

That's the worst way to hear about the death of a friend. A voice on the telephone.

'You knew Dan O'Neill, didn't you? Haven't you heard? They found the body this morning.'

'What?' you scream, but she takes no notice, full of her own importance at breaking the bad news. You feel dizzy and angry at the same time, black spots float in front of your eyes, and you hold on to the phone as if sinking.

'Overdose. Sleepers and booze, maybe deliberate, maybe accidental—they're not sure yet. There'll have to be a post mortem.'

And you're still trying to take it in. He wasn't just a casual acquaintance, you should be shouting; he was someone I loved, damn you, a soul mate, my greatest friend.

She knows he and I were lovers, and she knows that even though we broke up long ago, we are—were—still close friends, so close that we don't have to observe the conventions. She is enjoying being the first person to tell me that he is dead. Later she will boast about it: 'I was the one who told her; she hadn't heard.'

The voice continues, unaware of my silent fury.

'Of course in a way it was a mercy, what with his drinking and the cancer coming back—you knew, didn't you, that the cancer had come back? That's why he was so depressed. It's been a while since you've seen him then?'

Ah, she has me there.

Was it eight months or eighteen? Two bottles of Chardonnay

and a Chinese meal in a basement near Baggot Street, he morose, smoking slim panatellas between courses, scanning a crumpled *Evening Herald* he'd picked up in Doheny & Nesbitt's, grunting in answer to my attempts at conversation. His affectation of indifference to a world that he experienced too intensely had evolved into habitual churlishness. The dashing young poet had become an overweight, pale-faced blob of misery, self-destructing before my eyes.

Three weeks ago, only three weeks ago, he'd been in London. He rang me, it was already late, and he asked me to meet him for dinner at the Groucho. I could imagine it—a beer-stained *Evening Standard*, more grunts, more silence, more cheap cigar smoke.

No thanks. But I said I'd visit him in Dublin, which I kept putting off. I could have been there when it happened but, like so many of his friends, his so-called friends, I couldn't face his gloom. I didn't know the cancer had come back, if indeed it had. But even if I had known, I do not think it would have changed the way I behaved. He didn't want sympathy.

When he was back in Dublin, he sent me a postcard. On the back he wrote two lines from Thomas Wyatt, nothing else.

They fle from me that sometime did me seke
With naked fote stalking in my chambre.

It had been nearly twenty years since I'd stalked him in his chamber, but fair enough.

I couldn't face what I saw as his failure, his transformation from brilliant young poet to gossip-writer. Writing social gossip, tittle-tattle, recycling old stories, no piece longer than three column inches, while drinking and smoking himself to death. Do we not, to some extent, define ourselves by the friends we choose?

Thancked be fortune, it hath ben othrewise
Twenty tymes better . . .

'We are not going to get involved; I don't want to get involved . . .'

He was sitting on the side of the bed, naked, his head in his hands, faking despair. I was laughing:

'Don't get hysterical. We are involved, that's it, there's no point in fighting it.'

'But the timing! We've had only three nights together, and you're leaving tomorrow. It'll be weeks, maybe months before we're together again. What am I supposed to do while you're away?'

'Write me letters?'

'Letters, my arse. No, that would just make it worse.'

'You're right. I certainly don't want to spend my whole time away pining for you.'

'Okay. So until we're together again, same country, same room, same bed, we'll go on behaving like we did before we met.'

'What do you mean by that?'

'I can go on being a cynical bastard and you can be a cold, stuck-up bitch.'

'Love you, Dan.'

'Love you too, Ashling.'

That silenced us, saying it for the first time. The declaration, begun in jest, was true.

'Think of all the time we've wasted,' he said.

'I used to think you hated me. You were always so rude. And drunk.'

'Drunk, maybe. Rude, maybe. But I didn't hate you. I fancied you. You're beautiful. But such a fucking know-all.'

'I never saw the real you until I ran into you in the ABC Bakery in Fleet Street. That's when I first saw through the façade.'

'Every morning at eleven-thirty sharp, pub opening time, I disappear from the desk, and everyone thinks I've gone down to the Crossed Keys for a drop of the hard stuff. They give me these pitying looks: there goes the poor alcoholic, can't wait till lunchtime for his first shot.'

'Whereas in fact you are to be found in the ABC Bakery drinking black coffee and eating a doughnut.'

'Shush! You'll ruin my reputation!'

Back in the late seventies I went to Fleet Street once a week to deliver my copy to the paper where Dan worked on the features desk. We were part of a loose circle of Irish journalists, known as the Irish Mafia, or the Murphia—an example of what passed for wit on Fleet Street. 'Murphia, my arse,' Dan used to say when English colleagues made the joke.

I was a new arrival, fresh out of college, and the Mafia helped me to break into journalism. We met in pubs, at Irish Club bashes, embassy and tourist board launches, Saint Patrick's Day drinks, boozy Sunday lunch parties.

At weekends we often drank at Cassidy's in Notting Hill. Dan O'Neill lived nearby, and he was always there. He was tall and slim with curly black hair and large blue eyes, which makes him sound impossibly handsome. The reality also featured a bulbous nose, already in his mid-thirties reddened by drink, and a tendency to acne. He wore corduroy trousers and a Donegal tweed jacket in the winter, always with a white shirt and a narrow, dark tie. In summer he wore a well-cut lightweight suit in cream linen, dating from his New York days. He always looked neat, unlike the majority of male journalists. In spite of his writing talent, he was regarded as a bit of a buffoon, the quintessential drunken Irish journalist. Except for his accent: his parents had emigrated to Canada when he was in his teens, and his time in Toronto and then New York had left him with an accent that was more mid-Atlantic than Dublin. His language was foul, but he could tell a good joke, and had a reputation as a fiercely loyal friend—once he knew you.

You would never guess from the facade, but he also published poetry in small magazines. Journalism was just a money-earner. I once overheard him telling someone that poetry was his vocation, journalism was just a job, hackwork to pay the bills. I associated vocations with priests, and found the remark pretentious, pseudo-mystic. My traditional Catholic upbringing was followed by college at the height of the hippie movement (What's your star sign, babe?). I found both sets of belief equally ridiculous, and was a confirmed pragmatist who did not believe in anything she could not see.

I went to the launch of his first collection of poetry partly because the Mafia would be there, partly from curiosity. What sort of a poet was this awful person? I was dumbstruck when Dan read at the launch. The raffish man-about-town with his world-weary, seen-it-all air was replaced by a self-effacing character who read graceful, elegiac poems in an almost apologetic manner.

The next day, delivering the weekly book review to Fleet Street, I got off at the usual bus stop in front of the ABC Bakery, and although I had never been inside the place before, I was irresistibly tempted by the aroma of fresh coffee. And there, standing at the narrow ledge that served as a table for those eating in, was Dan O'Neill with a doughnut and a cup of black coffee.

I had been reading the poems on the bus, and I shoved the copy at him, gushing praise and asking for a signature.

'Only if you'll agree to have dinner with me.'

'Done.'

Which was how, two weeks later, we were lying in bed on the evening before my departure for west Cork. I was borrowing a house from a friend and intended to spend the next four months alone, writing.

'Why didn't you make a pass at me years ago?' I asked, curious to know, now that it seemed so obvious we were meant for each other.

'You hadn't read my poetry, and you were too busy being the Mafia's latest *wunderkind*. I hovered on the sidelines, watching.'

'You called me a dumb broad once in Cassidy's. Or was it a

dumb fucking broad?'

'The years I spent in New York learning my trade have left me with a weakness for coffee and doughnuts, and an offensive vocabulary which I cannot shake off. I love the furious reaction I get when I call someone a dumb broad. Women are always at their most beautiful when they are angry. Redheads, especially.'

'And two weeks ago? After I'd read your book? The day we met in the ABC and had dinner?'

'You ran away, if you remember. Ran away and jumped into a taxi.'

'Intuition. I was scared.'

The borrowed house was only an hour and a half from Cork Airport, and Cork was only an hour's flight from London. In one of those extraordinary coincidences that often attend the start of an affair, Dan had also been planning to spend some time away, writing. My borrowed house suited him perfectly. Now he could leave London sooner rather than later, but it would still take him a month or so to disentangle himself from work commitments.

'And I guess I'd better tell Marisa her days as my favourite dumb broad are numbered.'

I pretended to strangle him at the words 'dumb broad'. I knew Marisa from Cassidy's. She was a model, who had become a television actress, and certainly no dumb broad; she was great company, dry-witted and funny, nobody's fool.

'She used to be on the game, did you know that? I've been going with Marisa for years, and I still pay. She says it turns her on. But for God's sake don't spread it around.'

'Incredible.'

'So when do I get the bollocking?'

'What?'

'Aren't you jealous? She's a friend of yours.'

'If I got jealous of every woman you'd been with before I met you I'd go mad. Anyway, I don't believe in making promises at this stage. Let's take it easy, one step at a time.'

'I can't believe this is happening.'

'Me neither.'

My friend Stephen's house was right on the water's edge in a village on Roaring Water Bay. He said I would be doing him a favour by living there in winter, keeping the place aired, and being on the spot in case of storm damage.

I hired a car for the first week, while I settled in. The further I drove from the airport, the emptier the countryside became. The last touches of suburbia—street lighting, tidy gardens, pedestrian crossings—disappeared west of Bandon. The lack of people and traffic was both eerie and exhilarating.

I had been told to pick up the key at the bar opposite the house. The barman fished it out of a pint glass beside the wooden drawer that served as a cash register, and gave me an interrogating look.

'You're not from these parts originally?'

'No, Cork City. But I've been down here on holiday.'

'On your own, are you?'

'For the moment. I've a friend joining me in a few weeks' time.'

'It's a big house for one girleen.'

None of your business, I thought to myself. Girleen, for God's sake. Three years in London had left me out of touch and out of sympathy with rural ways.

Two hours later I admitted that maybe the barman had a point. The house was a large Victorian building. One of its gable ends had three bay windows, one above the other, projected out over the sea. It had been empty since August. The central heating fired up with a great whoosh and a stink of kerosene. All but two of the light bulbs were blown, the bed linen was muddled up in a heap, there was no soap and no toilet paper. Mice—or something bigger—had got into the kitchen and eaten their way through a packet of cornflakes right down to the cardboard, leaving droppings strewn on the floor and worktops. The only edibles were a bottle of tomato ketchup, a jar of marmalade and a tub of white pepper.

The central heating rumbled away as I set to work. I raided the local shop, which stocked an impressive range of useful things, including light bulbs, mousetraps and coal. Stephen had recommended the master bedroom, on the third floor of the seaward-facing gable end, for the view: 'Sleep with the curtains open, and it's almost as good as being at sea.'

Stephen had not mentioned the bed, a high four-poster hung with dark red curtains, with barley-twist pillars at each corner. The mattress was so far off the ground that a small, red-upholstered footstool was provided to help you in and out. I pulled back the blankets and spread heavy linen sheets open to air. Everything was chilly and damp, in spite of the heating now blasting out from big old-fashioned radiators, accompanied by loud clanks and gurgling.

I wiped the last traces of scouring powder from the kitchen floor, but could not face cooking. I had been working non-stop for three hours. I opened a packet of ham, and ate it straight from the fridge, then I headed over to the pub.

This time I remembered my manners, and introduced myself to the barman, Willie. An old man in a greasy cap farther up the bar had his hands around a steaming glass of pink liquid. Hot port! It had been the favourite tipple of my great-aunt, and it was exactly what I needed at that moment. The heat—or the alcohol—went straight to my toes and back up to my cheeks, giving me a warm glow that neither central heating nor floor scrubbing had produced.

One hot port led to another, as regular customers drifted in. Willie kindly introduced 'the girleen who's staying in Stephen's house' to a series of individuals, both locals and blow-ins—as incomers were labelled. Hot port and 'girleen', which nobody had called me since I was a child, made me feel as if I had fallen into a time warp.

I don't know how many drinks were bought for me, only that it became harder and harder to follow the conversation. My new acquaintances seemed to be hiding something from me, making obscure references to Stephen's house. The old man in the greasy cap said something I did not catch, which sent the company into peals of laughter.

Willie interpreted the old man's question for me: 'He says the last fellow to stay in that house alone ran out to the street in his pelt in the middle of the night, and he wants to know will you do the same, because he'd hate to miss it.'

The joke seemed even funnier to the company the second time around. In spite of the port fumes fuddling my head, I started to get the message.

'You mean Stephen's house is supposed to be haunted?'

'No "supposed to be" about it, girleen. I wouldn't spend a night in there alone if you paid me a thousand pounds. Nor would anyone else around here.'

'Well I don't believe in ghosts, so you needn't hang about to see if I do a midnight flit. I'm going back right now, and I intend to sleep like a log. Goodnight.'

My exit was marked by a not-unkind mock cheer. I staggered when the fresh sea air hit me, and was glad no one had followed me out to notice. I was both angry and drunk, a bad combination. If there is one thing I dislike about rural Ireland, it is superstition. Ghosts, my arse, as Dan would say.

I did not sleep like a log, at least not at first. I lay on my back listening to the sea, lapping gently against the sea wall. Stephen had designed the curtains of the bed so that they could be pulled back to each of the four corners to lessen the sensation of being entombed. I left them half-closed. I liked the cosiness. I closed the door to the landing, just in case the vermin that had eaten the cornflakes packet were still at large.

I nodded off, the way one does after several hot ports, but woke about two hours later needing a pee. It took a little time to remember where the bathroom was. The door creaked as I went out on to the landing, and a floorboard cracked, contracting after the sudden blast of heat.

Back in bed, I could hear the sea livening up. A storm was gathering, and a new series of creaks and bangs woke me with a jolt every time I was about to nod off. When I checked my watch, I realised I must have been lying on my back with my eyes wide open, listening to the sea for over an hour.

I closed my eyes and tried that yoga technique of concentrating on all the sounds inside the room, then moving your consciousness to all the sounds outside the room. It usually sends me off to sleep within minutes.

I was just about to doze off when the door, which I had left closed, creaked open. There was a slight commotion near the far right-hand bedpost. Someone was muttering, a rustle of paper, more muttering.

I froze, terrified. Not rats. Definitely not rats. Bigger than rats.

An intruder? If I screamed would anyone hear me? Could I scream?

The source of the noise moved across the end of the bed. Now it was near the parting in the curtains on my left-hand side. I acted dead, trying not to give away my presence by breathing. I had broken out in a cold sweat and was numbed by panic. Someone sat on the edge of the bed, then a body slid under the sheet, a blessedly familiar body, with breath that smelt of whiskey and cheap cigars. The panic evaporated and was replaced by confusion.

'Dan? You're not supposed to be here.'

'Don't worry. I only want to hold you. I've been missing you.'

'I missed you too, but you're not supposed to be here, you can't be—'

'Shut up you dumb broad.'

It was Dan all right.

We fitted our bodies together, my head on his shoulder, my feet under his, in the way that had become so familiar in our short time together, and we slept.

I woke up a while later and ran my fingers through his soft curly hair and over the cool skin of his back. It was definitely Dan.

I regained all my waking logic. The one thing I feared was that at some point Dan would wake up and want to make love. That would prove it was not a dream—surely I could tell the difference between making love and having an erotic dream—and the story of how he'd got there would have to be told.

I knew it was impossible for Dan to be there, physically impossible. I had taken the last flight of the day from Heathrow to Cork, and he was not on it. But here he was. So how could I explain it? And if I couldn't explain it, then it was all a dream—or a hallucination with physical manifestations, which meant that I was going mad.

I was too tired to go on trying to work it out. I decided to enjoy it instead. Dan moaned and kissed me on the neck.

'Ashling.'

I rolled over on top of him.

'Where the hell did you get this stupid bed?' His voice was slurred. Who's ever heard of a drunken ghost? A smashed-out-of-its-skull ghost? I started to laugh.

'It belongs to Stephen, the friend who leant me the house.'

'Oh, yeah, we're in west Cork. Listen! I can hear the sea, there's a storm coming up. How clever of you. Outlandish!'

He rolled us over so that he was on top.

'Christ! It really is Ashling!'

'I love you.'

'I love you.'

We came together and fell apart exhausted to lie holding hands.

It was then that I slept like a log.

When I woke, I lay with my eyes closed for a long time, hoping that he would still be there.

Not a trace. Not even a whiff of whiskey and cheap cigars.

When Willie in the pub enquired, I said I liked the house. It was a bit strange at first, and no, I didn't sleep too well. But I blamed that on the storm, which had indeed been mighty.

What else could I have said? The truth was too bizarre to reveal—weird if it was a ghost, which it couldn't be because I didn't believe in ghosts—weird if it was not. I didn't want to tell anybody. When Dan rang me that evening from London, I didn't mention it.

I expected, even half-hoped, that it might happen again, but the next night, and every night after I slept perfectly well, unaccompanied by any presence, ghostly or physical. The vermin never reappeared, and I quickly got used to sleeping so near to the sea. I settled into my work routine.

Dan arrived four weeks later. It was dark by the time he got to the house. We went straight to the sitting room where we made love on a rug in front of the open fire, drinking duty-free whiskey, exchanging news, and laughing. I dozed off briefly and woke to find Dan staring into my face. He was clinging to me and he whispered: 'Promise me something, Ashling?'

'What?'

'Promise me you'll never leave me?'

'I'll never leave you. Never. I love you.'

'My Ashling.'

I stopped whispering and said in a deliberately casual voice, 'Tell me something. Just out of interest. What were you doing the night I left London?'

'The night you left London. Why?'

'At about three in the morning of the night I left?'

'You're not going to like this.'

'Go on.'

'It was only the one time.' He stopped being defensive and

sounded contrite. 'I went to Cassidy's the night you left. I took a bottle of whiskey home and next thing I knew I was in a taxi on the way to Marisa's, and it was about half-three in the morning. I paid her twenty quid to pretend to be you.'

'Was she any good?'

'Too good. I really thought it was you. But there were these hallucinations, I kept thinking we were in some amazingly high four-poster bed with curtains, and the bed was in west Cork, and I kept hearing the sea, like out there . . . I mean, a sea storm coming up in Kensington: I must have been in the horrors!'

I sat up, suddenly chilled.

'Follow me,' I said, and led him upstairs to the bedroom.

My Heart Aches

'*MY HEART ACHES and a drowsy numbness pains/my senses . . .*'

'Sense. Singular.'

'*Pains my sense as though of hemlock I had drunk or emptied some dull opiate to the dregs . . .*'

'Drains, drains. Oh, come on!'

'Okay. Drains. Drains. *One minute past . . .*'

'No full stop. *Emptied some dull opiate to the drains/One minute past*—drains to rhyme with pains—pains, drains, remember?'

'Right. Pains, *drains*, drunk, *sunk* . . . now I'm getting there:

My heart aches and a drowsy numbness pains

My sense as though of hemlock I had drunk

Or emptied some dull opiate to the drains

One minute past and Lethe-wards had sunk . . .'

Neither Fiona nor Francesca said what both were thinking: in the whole morning Fiona had memorised only the first four lines of eight ten-line stanzas. Her father had promised her a twenty-pound note if she had the whole poem off by the end of the summer term: eighty often impenetrable lines. He had learnt it as a fifteen-year-old schoolboy, he still recited it on occasion as his party piece: now it was her turn. Twenty pounds was a lot of money in 1965: Francesca's dress allowance was considered generous at five pounds a month. Impressed by the magnitude of the challenge, Francesca, who wanted to be an actress and was used to learning lines off by heart, promised to hear her best friend.

'I will be your *répetiteur*,' she said, in her most gracious tone of voice.

'Shouldn't that be *répetiteuse?*' Fiona asked, raising her right eyebrow.

They were both confident of passing French O level next year, but feared they would fail Latin, for they had perfected a method of cheating on tests by hiding the textbook under their desks and sneaking it out for a judicious peep while kind Miss Malcolm's frail, elderly back was turned. Failing Latin would be a disaster, as without it, they would not be eligible to apply for a place to read English at Oxford.

'Tis not through envy of thy happy lot,

But being too happy in thy happiness—oh, for goodness' sake, make up your mind, poet!' Fiona was not a great fan of Keats in the normal course of events. She was more a Robert Frost kind of person, stopping by woods on a snowy night, taking the lesser trod of two paths, that was her kind of thing. But her father wanted the bloody *Nightingale*, so *Nightingale* it was.

'They think I'm dim. They think I can't do it, that's why I must. It's not just the twenty pounds.'

'I know,' said Francesca, 'I know, I know, I know.' She had seen Fiona's father look at his eldest daughter as if she were a mildly amusing clown. He could not see the beauty she had become, with her Byzantine profile and long black hair. Fiona's father was a lawyer and a businessman, head of a large multi-national company, who mingled with the crème de la crème from the world of diplomats, bankers and politicians. Tall and dark-haired, he wore waistcoats embroidered with tapestry, used a monocle and took snuff. Once he gave the two girls a pinch of snuff each and laughed at their sneezes and weeping eyes.

'Tis not through envy of thy happy lot?' Fiona was the piggy in the middle of a large family, with three elder brothers and three younger sisters, and generally assumed to be of below-average intelligence, by McNair family standards. The McNair males were all barristers (with the possible exception of the eldest son, Christopher, who had just been sent down from Oxford, the less said the better, according to Mrs McNair); their wives were

well read, passionate about art history and architecture and formidably energetic, as well as being flamboyant but thrifty managers of large households. In the past, their daughters would have done the season, and been presented at court as debutantes, but since the war, according to Mrs McNair, now that there was no court presentation, only *nouveaux riches* did the season.

'*But being too happy in thy happiness,*
That thou light-wingéd Dryad of the trees,
That thou light-wingéd Dryad of the trees . . .'
'*In some melodious plot!* It's the first of those short lines. Plot to rhyme with lot, remember? Bloody nonsense if you ask me, how can a plot be melodious?'
'*That thou light-wingéd Dryad of the trees,*
In some melodious plot
Of beechen green and shadows numberless,
Singest of summer in full-throated ease.'
'Okay, Piglet, that's enough for today. One stanza a day, this week and next, with weekends for revision and Wednesdays off, then the third week we put it all together for a series of run-throughs and a dress rehearsal.' Besides being piggy-in-the-middle in her family, Piglet snorted when she laughed, hence the nickname.

Wednesdays were off because on Wednesday school finished at lunchtime, with the afternoons left free for outdoor exercise or museum visits. Fiona and Francesca generally spent their Wednesday afternoons in a cinema on the Fulham Road.

'Thanks for the Wednesdays off, I really appreciate that.'
'Got to rest the brain, Piglet.'

There was one word in the poem that puzzled them. Francesca suspected it was Greek, so Fiona consulted Miss Malcolm. Miss Malcolm often warned them of the difficulties that lay ahead in the form of Greek, should they choose to study Classics.

'Hippocrene!' she said. 'You must be reading Keats?'

'I'm memorising *Ode to a Nightingale*. For a bet with my father.'

'*O, for a beaker full of the warm South,/Full of the true, the blushful Hippocrene?*'

'Exactly. *With beaded bubbles winking at the brim,/And purple-stainèd mouth;*'

'Hippocrene is poetic shorthand for the source of all inspiration. The Hippocrene was a fountain on Mount Helicon, sacred to the muses. From the Greek, *hippos*, horse and *krene*, fountain, fountain of the horses, created, according to legend by a strike of the hoof of Pegasus.'

'The hoof of Pegasus!'

'Used, of course, metaphorically: by drinking from the fountain of the muses the poet seeks to heighten his poetic powers. *That I might drink and leave the world unseen,/And with thee fade away into the forest dim.* I take it that you are acquainted with Bacchus?'

'Oh yes, my brother is an expert on Bacchus.'

To enhance her powers of memory, Fiona had written the whole poem out in her own hand in a hardback notebook. She carried the notebook with her everywhere, and read the Ode in all her empty moments: during break, in the bus queue, on the bus, before and after tea. If she was having nursery tea with her younger sisters, known as the smallies, she read it aloud to them, to practise the sound of it. She read the day's allotted stanza first thing in the morning, and last thing at night she ran through the poem as far as today's stanza silently in her mind, then read the whole poem through to the end before falling asleep.

Her brother Christopher, who was hanging around at home, apparently with nothing to do, noticed her preoccupation.

'Father has promised me twenty pounds if I can recite it for him.'

'Twenty pounds! That would come in handy. I nearly know if off myself, I've heard him do it so often. What are you going to do with the money?'

'A long weekend in Paris, perhaps,' said Fiona, hoping to sound like a man of the world.

'Will you take me with you? We'd have the greatest fun!'

'I'll have to bring Francesca too. She's being incredibly helpful.'

'The more the merrier! We'll stay at a little hotel I know, not far from the hotel where Oscar Wilde died.'

'The one with the wallpaper? It's either me or the wallpaper, one of us must go?'

'How do you know that?'

'I've been rooting in your library while you were at Oxford. No, seriously, Francesca and I did a project on Oscar last year. Why did they send you down?'

'Because they're a load of silly idiots. The less said the better.'

'That's what mother says.'

'For once, mother is right.'

Stanza III, recited with high drama, *rallentando*, was their favourite so far. Francesca could not resist joining in, creating a rousing duet: *Fade far away, dissolve, and quite forget/What thou among the leaves hast never known,/The weariness, the fever and the fret/Here, where men sit and hear each other groan; . . .'* Then they would groan awhile, before Francesca raised the whip and Fiona continued: '*Where palsy shakes a few, last, sad gray hairs . . .'*

'Sad, last! *A few sad, last gray hairs.'*

'*Sad, last, gray hairs,/Where youth grows pale and spectre-thin, and dies;'*

Here Francesca joined in again for more of her favourite lines, and they chorused together tragically: '*Where but to think is to be full of sorrow/And leaden-eyed despairs . . .'*

It was Thursday of week one, *Fade far away, dissolve and quite forget* day. The school needed flowers for the Fourth Year's Open Day presentation. Fiona volunteered her mother's roses. The headmistress rang Mrs McNair, and it was arranged that Fiona and her friend Francesca would travel to the McNair home by bus on their lunch break to collect several bunches of hybrid tea roses. Mrs McNair's son Christopher would pick them. 'As soon as they are big enough to walk, all my children are shown how to pick roses. Fiona and her friend can have a bite of lunch with Christopher, who will be on his own. I have a luncheon engagement, or I would deliver the flowers myself. Please make sure that the girls have their bus fare.'

There was a long wait at South Kensington for the bus, but the girls didn't mind. To be out of school on a sunny summer midday with the prospect of lunch alone with Christopher was a treat.

'My parents like you because you speak in complete sentences,' said Fiona as they waited.

'So do you.'

'I know. But they don't notice. They think I'm thick and that's that.'

'I wish they'd let you try for Oxford, when the time comes.'

'They won't. Because I'm a girl. Girls don't go to Oxford, girls go to Paris for a year to learn French and *Cordon Bleu* cookery. Then they go to Florence for a year to learn Italian and the history of art. I'm setting an example for the smallies. If I were allowed to go to Oxford, they'd all want to go to Oxford.'

'And no one would learn *Cordon Bleu* cookery. I see the problem.'

'You can laugh and be sarcastic! You've got nice parents who give you a dress allowance as well as pocket money, and let you have your hair cut.'

Fiona was not allowed to cut her hair for another year, until 1966 when she would be sixteen. It was a family tradition, according to her mother, handed down from the previous generation along with Nanny, who made all of Fiona's clothes apart from her winter coat, which was run up by Mr McNair's tailor. Francesca had petitioned Mr and Mrs McNair on Fiona's behalf, and explained how a dress allowance worked, and how much nicer Fiona would look if she were allowed to cut her hair and shop in the High Street like all her friends.

'What does your father do, Francesca?' asked Mrs McNair, in a kind tone of voice.

'He's an architect. And my mother is a magazine editor.'

'That explains it. In this house we are very traditional. We like Fiona to look as she does, to look like a schoolgirl, while that is what she is.' She paused here to look at Francesca's geometric pageboy bob, her above-the-knee corduroy skirt and her skinny rib sweater. 'Plenty of time for dressing up later in her life. It's not a question of money, obviously, it's the thin end of the wedge. That's what a dress allowance would be, the thin end of the wedge.'

In other words, thought Francesca, give Fiona a taste of freedom and she will start insisting on other rights, like a decent education beyond the age of sixteen. She knew instinctively not to start arguing the case with the McNairs. She felt so strongly about it that she would fail to speak in sentences.

The biggest mystery, as she remarked to Fiona, was why such an old-fashioned couple had chosen to send their daughter to a school with no uniform and a reputation for progressive education.

'Well, quite simply, because they didn't want to send me to boarding school, and it was the nearest girls' school to our house,' said Fiona. 'Only five stops on the bus. And some of their friends send their daughters there, and like it. That was all they knew about it. Before me, they'd only ever had boys, and the boys automatically went to my father's schools.'

Fiona solved the dress allowance impasse by raiding the dressing-up box, choosing a pair of elfin suede ankle boots with a fringed cuff, and a jewel-coloured hand-woven poncho. With her black hair hanging straight down her back, she blended in perfectly with the new wave of exotically attired youth who were starting to appear in the streets of London.

The two girls got off in Kensington High Street and walked around the corner to the McNairs' large detached house. The front door was on the latch, and a heap of long-stemmed roses in tidy bunches were piled on the hall table. Christopher was discovered in the dining room, seated at a highly polished mahogany table, in front of a bottle of wine on a silver coaster, and a silver platter containing cold roast chicken.

'What kept you?' he called. 'I opened a bottle of rosé in your honour, and it's nearly gone already.'

'The bus,' said Fiona, directing Francesca to her place and pushing the chicken in her direction. Christopher, meanwhile, pulled another cork and filled the girls' glasses.

'I take it that you are acquainted with Bacchus?' said Fiona. The Latin teacher's question had already become a family joke, a welcome distraction at the increasingly tense meal times.

'Thought you'd appreciate a beaker full of the warm South,' said Christopher. '*Full of the true, the blishful Hippocrene.*'

'Blishful?' said Fiona, snorting, and Francesca laughed so hard she sprayed pink wine all over her chicken.

'Blissful, then,' said Christopher, not at all embarrassed by his gaffe.

'Blushful!' the scholars shouted, holding out their beakers for more.

Christopher offered them a toast: 'Days of wine and roses!'

'*Though the dull brain perplexes and retards,*' said Fiona. 'The first four lines are easy, because they rhyme a b a b—thee, pards, poes-ie, retards. But then you get three lines without a rhyme, the blasted short line, and then the last two that rhyme, fair enough, but they are so far away from the lines they rhyme with that by then I've forgotten what they were, so it's no help.'

'*Nil desperandum*, Piglet, *nil desperandum.*'

Fiona knew from the tension around the table at breakfast and dinner not to persist with her questions about Christopher and

Oxford. It was very much *pas devant les enfants*, and in this matter she was apparently still *un enfant*. Therefore, when she was at the table her parents did not harangue poor Christopher, so she stayed there stubbornly, through the coffee and liqueurs, even though she was normally allowed to excuse herself after the pudding and go to do her homework. That night she lingered on the stairs long enough to hear a murmured suggestion from her mother that perhaps his tutor was to blame, and should be pursued, and a hissed reply from her father: 'Do you expect me to play the Marquess of Queensberry? Threaten to horsewhip him? This is 1965 my dear, not 1895!'

Christopher, uncharacteristically, said nothing, but stared ahead of him at the cruet, as he had all evening.

'Some of them are easier than others, that's what it is,' said Francesca kindly, after Fiona had failed again to get beyond the first two lines of the next stanza:
   '*I cannot see what flowers are at my feet,*
   Nor what soft incense hangs upon the boughs . . . *hangs upon the boughs*'
   '*But,*' said Francesca, 'It has to be "but", you can see it coming!'
   '*But in embalmèd darkness, guess each sweet*
   Wherewith the seasonable month endows . . . *wherewith the seasonable month endows* . . .
   '*The grass, the thicket and the fruit-tree wild;*—it runs on, it's more like a five-line intro than a four-line one in this stanza . . . then the list goes on. Not one of his finest I would say.'
   'Reminds me of that bit of that Shakespeare we had to learn in first year. *I know a bank whereon the wild thyme grows* . . . I'd never felt such despair as I did that evening. I thought I'd never, ever get it off by heart, even when I noticed the rhymes, they didn't seem to help . . .'
   'But you did it, we did it, remember?'
   'Yes, we did. And I can still recite it to this day.'

'So you can do this too. Treat it like a list—grass, thicket, fruit tree, hawthorn, eglantine, violets, musk-rose . . .'

'Then more wine, The coming musk-rose full of dewy wine/ The murmurous haunt of flies on summer eves.'

'Musk-rose, wine, flies'—definitely not his finest hour.

'Reminds me of Christopher. You know how proud mother was of her new car?'

'The green mini-shooting brake? With real wood on the back? That she takes up to the market in Goldhawk Road every Friday?'

'A complete write-off. Christopher, late at night, yesterday, full of dewy wine, I can only assume . . . Not badly hurt, just cuts and bruises and a gammy knee.'

'Do you ever wonder why he's so accident-prone?'

'Mother suggested sending him to Florence with a small allowance. Something about getting it out of his system.'

'So what did your father say?'

'He glared at her across the table, glared like this, and he hissed, he really hissed: "You would make a *remittance man* of my son and heir?" As if it was something really terrible, the absolute worst ever.'

'A remittance man?'

'Yes. Never heard of it before. Something to do with his being sent down from Oxford, and 'the love that dare not speak its name'. Remember last year, when we were doing that project on Oscar Wilde?'

'I remember the trouble we had with sodomy. What was it the dictionary said, an unnatural form of sexual intercourse, esp. that of one male with another? When we were only getting used to sexual intercourse being natural, that totally animal *thing* being what your parents did to make a baby, or in your case seven babies, too bizarre among civilised people, so what on earth was an unnatural form of it? Remember when we looked up sodomite, hoping for more information, and what did we get?'

'"One who practises or commits sodomy". A fine distinction, practising or committing. But it's still no help with a remittance man, is it?'

'God knows what a remittance man is! I'd say we're on safer ground with "the love that dare not speak its name", you know where you are with that. Let us hope your dear brother is spared the fate of a remittance man. Now, back to work, take it again from the top: 'I cannot see what flowers . . .'

The fifth stanza was the turning point. Once Fiona had mastered that, the next three were easy: *Darkling I listen; and for many a time/I have been half in love with easeful Death . . . The voice I hear this passing night was heard/In ancient days by emperor and clown . . .* and finally, the great unanswerable question: *Was it a vision, or a waking dream?/Fled is that music: do I wake or sleep?*

There was a court case pending, and it would be ugly. In order to avoid the publicity, and the shame it would bring on his family, Christopher chose exile in Tuscany. He had always loved Italy, he explained to Fiona as he said goodbye.

'I am not running away from anything, I am running towards a new life with Stephen. We are going to farm saddleback pigs and grow herbs and vegetables in the Tuscan hills, far from "the weariness, the fever and the fret/Here where men sit and hear each other groan; where palsy shakes a few, last, sad gray hairs . . ."'

'Sad, last, sad last, get it right!'

She walked away, hoping he had not seen the tears in her eyes.

A week later, during a house party at the McNairs' country estate, after dinner, Fiona, wearing one of her father's frilly-fronted dress shirts under a dark red velvet jerkin from the dressing-up box, recited all eight stanzas of *Ode to a Nightingale*, loudly and clearly, word perfect. She had wanted Francesca to be there, but her mother explained apologetically that because Christopher had already left for Italy, an extra female at table had not suited the *placement*. Her three younger sisters, who had been allowed to watch from the minstrels' gallery, clapped their hands at the familiar last line, startling some of the guests, who had struggled to stay awake during the long recitation. Her father stood, shook her hand and smiled at her, scrutinising her face briefly through his monocle, as if for the first time.

The next morning Fiona found a twenty-pound note in an envelope under her napkin ring. She placed the note carefully in her leather wallet, one of Christopher's cast-offs. On Monday she would deposit it in her Post Office Savings Account, and forget about it for several years. It didn't matter: the project had been a total failure. She had not convinced her father that she was brilliant. Oxford was out of the question; there was no point in even asking. She knew that because of the words she had overheard the night before, as her father pointed one of his guests towards the splendid flying staircase that led up to the bedrooms: 'Yes, lucky girl, Fiona. She has the McNair knack of memorising poetry. Her party piece will come in very useful in Paris next year.'

Lucky, not clever. As she left the breakfast table she dreamt of Oxford for one last time. Then, in a spirit of fact, not of self-pity, she resigned herself to her fate, consoling herself, as she would do so often in the years to come, with the poet's immortal words: 'My heart aches'.

Coo

My father was the keeper of the Eddystone Light
And he slept with a mermaid one fine night
The fruits of this union they were three
A walrus, a porpoise, and then there was me . . .
Yo ho ho-oo! The wind blows free!
Oh, for a life on the open sea . . .

MY NAME IS Bill, Captain Bill, but my pals in Cork always
call me Coo. It's my accent, or more like a kind of a habit I've
got—coo!—it's what I say when I like something or when I'm
surprised. Nobody ever thought it strange in Hampshire where
I grew up. I suppose they all say coo all the time, I wouldn't
know, it's years and years since I've been home.

My father really was the keeper of the Eddystone Light, in
the days when it still had a keeper. I was born in Lymington and
based on the Hampshire coast most of my life. Until the day I
delivered a yacht from Southampton to Cork. It was the worst
passage I'd ever made, and I'd had some bad ones by then, coo,
I was no chicken. The rudder broke, the engine failed, then the
auxiliary engine failed, a gale blew up and I lost my bearings. I
was awake for three days and three nights. The third night I saw
a crew of gorgeous naked women scrubbing down the decks
and I thought my hour had come. I knew the old superstition,
the one that says if you're going to go at sea, the last thing you
see is some beauty calling you like that. They was waving at me,
asking me to join them out on deck and I was tempted, coo, I

can tell you, but I knew it was only a trick: I go out there and I'm done for.

I don't remember making a landfall, but I did, and I slept. When I woke up to blue skies and calm seas, tied up alongside at the foot of a wooded hill I thought coo! I've died and I'm in heaven! As it happens, I was at East Ferry on Cork Harbour, and there I stayed.

Coo had been around for about ten years when I first met him. I noticed this gaunt figure on the corner barstool, always in a blue and gray check shirt, always sockless in a pair of well-weathered dock-siders that told you straightaway he was a nautical man: the dock-siders, the faded skipper's cap, the full gray beard and the way that his blue eyes scanned the horizon through the window of Willie's bar every time something moved in the harbour. He must have been in his late fifties then. He wore an old-fashioned wristwatch on a thick leather strap which he sometimes took off and placed on the bar counter between his pint and his rolling tobacco. He spoke with a roundy Hampshire burr, which featured glottal stops and dropped haitches, characteristics that he assured me were common to all of the English south coast, not just the London area. To this rich combination he had now added the up and down lilt of the local accent.

His two front teeth stuck out so far that most of the time when his face was in repose, these blackened tusks rested on his lower lip. It gave him a comic look even at such highly charged moments as the lengthy pause which always followed one of his conversation openers:

'Did I ever tell you about the time that I was shipwrecked off Valparaiso?'

'The cold in Montreal is nothing compared to the cold in Murmansk.'

'I remember the night that the wind bent the lamp-posts on the prom in Alicante.'

He had travelled the world on cargo boats working for his

master mariner's ticket. When he got it, he took to combining yacht deliveries with skippering small boats, mainly, it seemed to me, for eccentric millionaires.

'Did I ever tell you about the geezer that asked what would happen if we turned left?'

She gave me that look again, like she was thrilled to listen to whatever tale I wanted to tell. She was a find, I tell you. Young, she was, thirty-one she told me when I asked, with long blonde hair, scrumptious figure, lovely sense of humour and not a bit stuck-up. As toothsome a morsel as I'd come across in many a long year. You could say I was sweet on her, but I knew it was never going to go anywhere. Mostly what happened was she listened, and I talked:

'He was a Pole, this geezer, can you believe? Made a killing in the rag trade and kept a beautiful sixty-foot motor cruiser in Southampton—cocktail bar, hot and cold running water, coo! I kept an eye on her for him, and the only time we ever took her out was the last two weeks in July. Every year I skippered him across to the Scilly Isles, and we pottered around the islands till it was time to go home again.

'Then one year, we're coming out of Southampton into the Solent as usual, and when it's time to turn to starboard for the Scillies he says to me "What would happen if we turned left?" I thought about it a bit, then I says, "If we turn left sooner or later we'll hit the Straits of Gibraltar and beyond that the Med." "Turn left!" says the geezer, and I didn't see the wife again for three whole years. Coo.'

The wife was not amused, and when he finally got back from the Med Coo packed his gear and set up base in a room above his local pub. Until the delivery trip to East Ferry.

Coo spent the summers working out of Kinsale and Crosshaven as a paid skipper for various yacht-owners. He skippered only for the best, and most of his clients became friends. Then I would be invited along for the weekend and I would do whatever I could in the way of crewing or cooking. We had three or was it four great summers. I got to know the coast between Crosshaven and Valentia with Coo. Everyone admired his expertise. He seldom seemed to use a chart or read the sailing directions; he seemed to acquire local knowledge by breathing the air.

In winter he worked as a general handyman or caretaker, often for the same people he skippered for in the summer. You never knew where he'd be based. A phone call would come through to Willie's bar and from the other end of a crackling line Coo would summon us to his nearest pub: 'Meet me in Newman's in Schull . . . meet me in the Blueloo Glengarriff . . . meet me in Billy's in Bantry,' and from there he would lead us to his current hideaway—a guesthouse shrouded in dust sheets or a luxurious waterside holiday home in sub-tropical gardens, and cook us a curry. He was a wonderful cook, and curries were his specialty. He never used curry powder, but mixed his own spices from a selection that he carried around in a Jacob's biscuit tin.

I didn't like the winters, not at all. There was no sailing and too much rain. I took any job I could get as long as it had accommodation with it because that way I didn't have to live in my caravan. The van was no good at all for my bronchitis, the walls ran with condensation as soon as I put the gas heater on. Every time I went back to the van, I ended up with this blasted non-stop cough.

But I never gave up the roll-ups, no matter how bad the cough got. I might cut back to five or six a day, but it was like I needed a fag to get me coughing. It was far, far worse without the fags.

I tried to explain this to her when I got back to Willie's bar—my pal in the village came good again with some live-in maintenance work. The cough was bad alright, but it looked worse than it felt. Finally, when I'd finished wheezing and

got my breath back and mopped up the tears with a bit of
handkerchief, I tried to explain it to her:

'Honest, love, it's not the fags that's the trouble. It's the
blasted damp, day in day out, rain rain rain rain rain. What
I need is a touch of the Pacific—the South Sea Islands, what
d'you say to that?'

My plan was for the two of us to work our way out there
doing deliveries and then stay on as a skipper and cook team.

'Cork to Miami; Miami to Panama; Panama to Galápagos;
Galápagos to Guayaquil; Guayaquil to Easter Island, Easter to
Pitcairn, Pitcairn to Tuamotu. Coo! Give it whirl, kid. What
have you got to lose?'

I was flattered by the invitation. Coo always preferred to sail
single-handed on long trips. It had always been my dream to
work my way around the world on small boats, but it was never
more than a remote dream, the occasional wild fantasy of every
weekend sailor. Now somebody was making me a serious offer.
But I was too stuck in the mud to accept. I hadn't had my job
long enough to get leave, and I had fought too hard for the
job to let it go. Coo gave me a chance to be different, to live
differently, and I turned it down.

It was around that time, mid-winter with dreams of the
South Seas, that Coo bought an ancient Ford Anglia for twenty-
five pounds.

'She won't win no beauty competition,' he said, 'but she's
got a roof rack and a tow-hitch. The tow-hitch alone is worth
twenty-five quid.'

The car meant he could return more often to base—base
being a dilapidated old caravan that he had parked in the garden
of a friend in East Ferry. The caravan was hard on his bronchitis
and we all started to worry about him. He was not even able for
a caretaking job that year. For the first time he agreed to go into
the local hospital and he also cut down to five roll-ups a day.

I let her persuade me to go into the hospital. I must have been feeling really low. My normal instinct is to run a mile when the word hospital is mentioned. And quite right I was too. As soon as they'd got me through the worst of the bronchitis, it was up to the Regional with me for a flaming X-ray and the news of a spot on my lung, a flaming big spot from the long-faced way they were carrying on. And then they wanted to take a bit out of me lung and send it to the lab to prove that I had what nobody wanted to mention—cancer. I let them do it, I decided I might as well know one way or the other while I was there, but I didn't tell any of the pals what was going on. Especially not her.

As long as I thought it was just the old bronchitis, the wet old winter, the damp getting into me, up until then I was grand. But once I knew it was cancer I turned really bad. Every so often I'd come over all queer with this pain in my chest, nothing like the bronchitis, nothing like anything you can imagine, and I'd be in a muck sweat and chewing my watchstrap to stop from screaming, curled over and doubled up with it. About once every forty-eight hours, and a little bit worse every time.

'We can't operate. I'm very sorry. It's too far advanced.'

'How long have I got?'

'Six months, maybe longer.'

'How much good time have I got?'

'That depends. Could be two or three months, could be a matter of weeks.'

I don't know why it came over me so strong, but I did not want her, or any of my Cork pals, to know what was going on. I never could take sympathy. The sympathy, the looks they'd give each other, the talk that would go on behind my back, the kindness and the consideration, all of that was far worse to me than the disease. I didn't want to be a burden to them.

So I invented Betty.

He met Betty the week he got out of the hospital. It was a bit of a whirlwind romance. Really! At his age! He'd met her in

Midleton where he was doing his weekly shopping. Just the way he said her name, Bet-ty, lingering over the two syllables, showed how badly smitten he was. There was no more talk of Valparaiso, Montreal, Murmansk or Alicante, no more invitations to Tuamotu. It was all Betty.

Betty was a blonde. Betty was 'a bit long in the tooth, but then I'm no chicken'. Betty was in Midleton to visit her mother, but Betty'd lived in London for the last thirty years. She had her own semi-detached house in Wembley. 'Her old man ran off with a bit of fluff—silly bugger.' Betty worked as a secretary with a firm of solicitors and she'd gone back because of her job before he'd had a chance to introduce us. Betty did not approve of his 'van'. She said that winters in the caravan were ruining his health. Betty said he should join her in Wembley straight away. Betty had central heating.

When he asked me for a loan of fifty quid—'Just enough for my ticket to Wembley and a spot of breakfast on the way'—I never dreamt of refusing. I didn't expect I would ever see it again, but I didn't care. He still looked desperately ill. That stay in hospital had really shaken him. Betty was probably the best thing for him.

I drove him to the ferry terminal at Ringaskiddy. No gangplanks here; a bleak sealed corridor stretched out beyond the 'Passengers Only' sign. Coo stopped and put down the old canvas kitbag he carried on his shoulder. I knew I was going to cry, and so was he from the look of him.

'Coo!' he said, 'I almost forgot!'

He took a set of car keys out of his pocket. 'She's in the car park at East Ferry. She's taxed and insured till the end of the month. The papers are in the glove compartment. I know you don't want her, so take her down to Willie's and sell fifty raffle tickets at a pound each. It's okay with Willie, I had a word. And don't look like it's the end of the world! I'll write to you from Betty's.'

Yo ho ho, the wind blows free
Oh for a life on the open sea.

Strangers

'IT'S ONLY TEN minutes over. They swim the cattle there.'

I didn't know the island, one of the smaller of the inhabited islands in Roaring Water Bay, and I was reluctant to go over in November. My informant, a retired vet, enumerated its attractions: 'No pub, no shop, no B&B or hostel. Not even a holiday home as far as I know. You'll love it. About a dozen permanent residents, most of them farming or fishing.'

It sounded promising. I was interested in taking photos of remote places that had not been affected by tourism, where you might get a glimpse of how people lived in the nineteenth century and earlier. Places where they swim the cattle across, for example. Places with ghost ridges where potatoes had been grown on every possible pocket of land, before the place was emptied by the blight.

There was a ferryman prepared to make the crossing for a small cash payment, Christy. I jotted down his mobile phone number, pleased that I would not have to spend the night on the island. I could just ring Christy when I wanted to come back. There were some advantages to modern technology. On the other hand, I would be missing the island dark. There is no dark like the dark of an offshore island at the westernmost extremity of Europe. In such a place, where light fades dramatically on a far horizon, you can take some remarkable photos.

Christy was waiting for me on the otherwise deserted pier, a paunchy middle-aged man in oilskins and a woolly hat. Blue paint was flaking off his boat, which had a small covered-in wheelhouse. I sat next to him on a ledge to one side of the wheel as the engine growled and spat then settled to a low, echoing putter. The island lay long and flat, parallel to the shore, with a hump at its eastern end. From this distance it seemed devoid of vegetation, but I could make out the gable-ends of a line of solidly built houses running along its spine. To the west the open sea stretched to the horizon, to the east the humps of other islands, the largest being the whale-like silhouette of Cape Clear.

Christy was an islander now living 'out', as he put it. He pointed to a lone concrete house on the hill above the pier, receding slowly from us. 'There would have been about three hundred people living 'in', up to the First World War. There was a school back then, but no doctor and no priest. They had to row over and walk two miles for Sunday mass. But there were a pub on the pier.'

'And today?' I asked

'Ten people in four households. Two families are still farming, and Timmy Mac does a bit of fishing.'

'What about the fourth family?' I asked.

'Strangers,' he said, sniffing and staring fixedly at the pier ahead to indicate that he was not saying any more.

'Ring me before dusk,' he said as he left me at the pier. 'You'll get a signal here, but not on the rest of the island.'

It was a dark autumn day, one of those gloomy half-lit days when the sun's light is hidden by layers of low cloud, and the sky seems to press down on your head. I walked first to the left, towards the nearer, eastern end of the island, ducking under a barbed wire fence and walking though a flock of sheep when the tarmac road ran out. The island grass was thick and springy underfoot, making me want to tear off my boots and go barefoot, like the island children long ago. There was a seal's head bobbing about twenty metres offshore in the little cove that marks the end of the island. He seemed to be watching me, curious. I took a few shots of him, then put the camera away in my backpack, suspecting rain.

The island is long and narrow, with no trees, only stunted bushes, carved into leaning shapes by the wind. The wind from the Atlantic sweeps down the length of the island, howling as it passes through the fencing wires. There is very little shelter, most of it man-made, the ruined gable ends of old stone-built houses, facing into the prevailing wind.

A few red bell-flowers clung to a misshapen fuchsia bush, along with some blackened wind-burnt leaves. A tiny bird, a wren most likely, gave short whistling calls from within, flying from branch to branch, invisible to my eye. I remembered sucking the honey from fuchsia flowers on sunlit childhood holidays.

The foreshore was brown with seaweed, pockmarked with limpets, teeming with sprats and crabs, serried ranks of mussels clinging to the old pier. A very old woman in Ballydehob told me that during the Great Hunger, when the potato crop failed, people tried to survive on seaweed and shellfish gathered on the strands of Roaring Water Bay. By 1847, after two years of crop failure, it was said that there was not a scrap of seaweed left on the shoreline from Roaring Water Bay to Cork.

When the wind died down, the silence was total. I had not seen another person since landing, but I could sense souls lingering. It was the silence of all those who had been born on the island, went to school there and were now gone, their ghosts hovering about the place where they should have lived.

I liked the feeling, a sensation that I call a slippage, when some part of your being slips into another time, joins the ghosts of another age, then slips back into this world, mildly disoriented and perhaps a little wiser. It had happened to me only days before at the huge fair in Maam Cross in Connemara that sprawls along the main road for several miles, stalls of dry goods, small groups of calves or sheep in pens, horses ridden bareback showing their paces in the fields alongside, patient donkeys tethered to road signs. It was dusk on another rainy day, and I glimpsed a stall displaying jewel-coloured Indian silks in the light of a paraffin lamp, the handsome dark-skinned vendor talking in a foreign tongue to his companion, and for a moment I was another person from another age, with different worries and woes, penniless in Connemara, trying not to panic at my lack of prospects, staring open-mouthed at the beautiful bright colours. Then I came back to reality, camera in hand, shaken.

After returning to my starting point near the little pier, I headed for the more exposed western end of the island. As I walked, dark clouds came scudding in from the northwest, driven by an ice-cold wind, and released a downpour of cold rain that ran off my weatherproof jacket and soaked my jeans.

There were ruined houses at intervals all along the road, but none of them had much roof left to give me shelter. There was only one inhabited house that I could see, freshly whitewashed, with smoke coming out of its chimney. As I ran past, laughing to myself in that strange exhilaration that sudden extreme weather can bring on, a girl with long blonde hair appeared at the front door, and beckoned me in.

'Hallo, my name is Melinda. What's yours?' She had a beautiful voice, piping, as if she were playing notes on a recorder.

'Rachel.'

'I have a friend called Rachel. She lives near my friend Audrey. Would you like to come in?'

I took off my wet jacket and left it hanging in the porch. 'Thank you so much. That's a heavy shower.'

Melinda smiled shyly. The house was warm and dry, the open fire recently lit, and she seemed to be alone. She was tall, almost as tall as me, but had the bland, unformed face of a young child. It was round, with pink cheeks, protuberant blue eyes, and a straight line for a mouth. Her blonde hair hung down her back, adding to the doll-like impression. She was wearing a thick red sweater and jeans. I assumed this was the house of strangers that Christy had mentioned.

'You don't sound like a native. Where do you come from?' I

hoped I sounded friendly, not too inquisitive. Her accent was definitely not local, but neither was it easy to place.

'Nowhere really. We've lived all over, so many places I can never remember them right. My grandad was with the Irish Lights, but now there's no more lighthouse keepers so he does odd jobs. Painting, decorating, plastering. He keeps a car on the mainland so he can get to the jobs. My granddad can do anything.'

'What about your parents?'

She shrugged. 'Grandad says I'm better off with him. And I am most of the time. Except when it rains for days and days. Then I get bored.' She sighed deeply, as she looked out at the rain, still coming down in rods. 'I'll make some tea. Then if it stops raining, I'll show you my garden, and we can go and visit Audrey and Rachel.'

It stopped raining as suddenly as it had started, and after tea Melinda showed me her garden. She had cleared a strip along the front of the house about a metre wide, and divided it into four squares. Each square was intricately patterned with stones: round black stones of a certain size, and smaller pure white ones. Bigger stones in golden sandstone formed the borders of the grid. The whole showed an extraordinary sense of pattern and design; not only that, the patterns in the squares were mirror images, white for black, of the next one. Melinda had resisted the obvious temptation to add wood, shells, cuttlefish and other objects found beachcombing, though these could be seen in a pile behind the house.

'That's my grandad's stuff,' she said, noticing I was looking at it. 'He keeps collecting it for me, but I don't want to use it. I like to keep things plain.'

'It's a beautiful garden, it's a work of art! Do you mind if I take some photographs of it?'

Then we walked to the strand, a few minutes beyond her house. I recognised the source of her pebbles, but also realised what extraordinary patience she must have to collect so many of such particular size and colour.

'Grandad says I should keep busy,' she said. 'I went strange when we lived near Leenane; he thinks that if I have a hobby it'll keep me cheerful.'

On one side of the strand was a tall rock face, with uprights that had been worn into free-standing figures by the tide, about the same size as the life-size statues of the Virgin Mary that you see in Catholic churches, their tops covered in weed, like hair. Melinda went up to the first of these, and gave it a smack. 'Wake up! Rachel! Rachel, I want you to meet Rachel!'

She giggled with delight, and pulled me by the hand. 'Go on, Rachel, say hallo to Rachel. Rachel can't talk, but you can.'

'Hallo, Rachel. My name's Rachel too.'

'And this is Audrey. Audrey looks very cross, but she's all right really, aren't you?'

'Hallo, Audrey.'

'Aren't you going to take a picture of my friends too?'

'Oh, yes, of course.' I was flustered, uneasy, and it must have shown. Her belief in their reality was disturbing. 'You stand with them, just there in front. Now, smile, and give me a wave!'

Back at the house, I met her grandfather, Johnny, who had just returned from the mainland. He was a gentle giant of a man, bearded with longish hair, well into his seventies, I guessed. He did not seem pleased that Melinda had company, and was silent to the point of hostility. I no longer felt welcome, and left shortly after, promising to send the photographs to Melinda.

When I saw the photographs of Melinda's garden I was even more impressed by its perfect and complex symmetry than I had been on the island. But even more intriguing, there was something very strange about the photos of Melinda and the rocks. When I printed them in high contrast black and white, Audrey and Rachel really did look like emaciated old women.

They immediately reminded me of the famine memorials that went up around Ireland in 1995, to mark the 150th anniversary of the tragedy.

I showed them to only two people, a friend who runs a gallery of contemporary art, and has a special interest in naïve art, and an arts journalist on a national daily who often followed up on unusual stories.

She must have been responsible, if only indirectly, but in the end I must accept full responsibility. A Sunday newspaper heard about Melinda, and put an investigative reporter on to the story. They got paparazzi shots of Melinda and her grandfather and splashed them all over the front page. They had done some digging: she was only twelve, but had never been to school, at least not in Ireland, and the man was not her grandfather.

As soon as I saw the Sunday paper, I drove down to the pier, and found the ferryman waiting. But Melinda and the man had already disappeared.

I ran from the ferry to Melinda's house. Half a dozen men in flak jackets, two of them carrying a large camera and a boom mike, were milling around in the road outside, trying in vain to get a signal on their mobiles. Melinda's garden had been scattered, deliberately kicked in all directions.

'It was like that when we arrived,' I was told, when I started roaring at them.

It was later confirmed that Melinda and the man had driven up to Rosslare and taken the ferry to Wales before an alert was issued. There had been no further sightings. The Gardai contacted me asking for copies of the photographs of Melinda, and I handed them over.

'Pity you didn't get a picture of the abductor,' they said, as sure as a court of law in their accusation. Melinda had a strong resemblance to a child who had gone missing while living in Greece with her hippy parents at the age of six. Now she had disappeared again.

I didn't go back to the island until the following autumn. Christy and I were like old friends by now.

'I always knew there was something not quite right about them. But she seemed happy enough, the creature. With her stones and that. But sometimes she came down to the pier, and asked me if I'd take her off the island. Said she was bored, nothing else, just bored. And fed up with the rain.'

'I know the feeling,' I said, looking at the sky. It was another leaky day.

'That's why I moved out,' said Christy, with feeling. 'Even now, every winter I think wouldn't it be nice to wake up somewhere else, with a blue sky and bright sunshine, and no ghosts cluttering up the road. I'll go too one of these days, I'm telling you, and it isn't Rosslare I'll be heading for.'

When I got to Melinda's house, it was as if her garden had never existed. The door of the house was hanging open, and the room was empty of furniture. Where once a bright fire had burnt, a puddle of rainwater stood.

I walked down one last time to the strand, and took comfort from the sight of Rachel and Audrey standing silently on the rocky foreshore as they had done since time immemorial.

A Shooting Incident in
County Tipperary

NOELEEN PARKED THE car half a mile from the house and opened the boot. It was a frosty, moonless night. She turned on the flashlight and slipped two cartridges into the breech of the shotgun. She put her gloves back on, closed the boot and walked off along the grass verge with the shotgun, still broken, under her arm. The grass was crisp under her feet. An owl hooted somewhere in the dark woods, startling her. She looked around for the dogs and then remembered that she had left them at home. Of course. The dogs and the children were sleeping.

There was only one cottage between the car and the gates of the big house. Christmas is cruel, she thought. The words provoked a rush of adrenaline. She could feel her heart, big, beating in her breast, beating in her throat. Cruel Christmas.

No lights at the cottage. Two in the morning. She knew the place where the Creevy Court wall had crumbled low enough for her to sit and swing her legs over instead of opening the squeaky cast iron gates. Once over, she crept under the rhododendron bushes, past the hydrangeas, onto the grass margin of the gravel drive.

It was a short, crescent-shaped drive leading to a large Victorian porch. Noeleen could hear herself breathing as she tried the porch's outer door. Locked. Unusually. Guilt? Fear? They were guilty and maybe they were afraid, afraid of her, so they had locked the doors. And where had they hidden his car? Supposing he wasn't there after all? But he was; he had to be. Where else could he be?

Feeling along the wall to the side of the house she found the corner and followed the wall of the house until she rounded another corner and came to the back door. Her boots made creaking noises on the gravel.

She tried the back door, turning the familiar knob. Locked. She leant on it, and pushed the top and the bottom to confirm that it wasn't bolted. Must not turn back at the first obstacle, resolution, keep going forward.

Shotgun clicked up and ready, butt dug deep into shoulder against trembling, rush of nausea, aim, close eyes, *shoot* the lock off, no stopping now, one cartridge left. Lights and a scream, rush through the door and up the stairs, she knew that scream, the top of the stairs, the landing, the bedroom door slammed shut, one kick and the bitch, naked, mouth gaping, hand reaching for something, oh, the point-blank pleasure, aim nicely, smiling slowly, take it easy, then the bitch, a shotgun now in her hand too, trigger click, bang, the deafening noise of it, all black, falling, finger still on trigger, warm blood falling on trigger finger, finger slipped, spraying an arc of shot, spraying shot up on ceiling, she down, blasted by the bitch.

A mother of six was killed in a shooting incident at Tarrantstown in County Tipperary in the early hours of St. Stephen's Day. The incident took place at Creevy Court, which was closed for business at the time. The state pathologist is travelling to the scene and a statement is expected later today. Creevy Court is owned by Miss Elaine Fahy who came to Tarrantstown from England a year ago and opened the house for bed and breakfast. The dead woman is believed to be local. Nobody else was injured in the incident, which is believed to have involved two licensed shotguns.

March 1988

Elaine Fahy bought Creevy Court with the money she had made out of her divorce from her second husband, Tim. They had no children, and the split was, as far as is possible, amicable. Tim and Elaine sold their house in Barnes at a nice profit, and divided the proceeds equally. Elaine changed back to her maiden name by deed poll, had auburn highlights added to her hair, and bought a large Victorian lakeside house just outside Tarrantstown, the village in County Tipperary where her mother had been born. She could never have afforded anything like it in England. She had bought a home and a business in one go. She believed that her late mother, an old-fashioned snob who had always hidden her humble origins, would have been overjoyed to see her daughter buying the big house, Major Coleman's place as it was in her day, even though she intended to run it as a bed and breakfast business. It was an upmarket venture, but trade all the same.

When Elaine had finished with the plumbers, the carpenters, and the housepainters, she put a card up in the local supermarket: 'Reliable help wanted for new B&B'. Elaine would serve the breakfasts herself on Major Coleman's Indian Tree china, but she did not intend to cook the breakfasts or wash up after them. Nor did she intend to strip and make the beds, nor do the laundry and the cleaning all by herself.

Noeleen O'Keefe was the first and only person to answer the ad, and she seemed ideal. She was the wife of a local car and tractor dealer, and appeared to be about Elaine's age—late thirties—and eager-to-please. Nothing was too much for her: she was a ball of energy, unstoppable:

'I've six children, the two youngest are already at the big convent, I can work full-time if you need me, Mrs Fahy, and give up the evening job in Barry's pub, but if it is only part-time help you're looking for, the pub job won't interfere with it at all.'

'It's Miss Fahy, not Mrs, but please call me Elaine.'

'And you call me Noeleen, now d'you hear?'

Noeleen O'Keefe was given the name Noeleen because she was born on Christmas Day. Her mother died of a sudden stroke on

St. Stephen's Day when Noeleen was twelve. She married Eddie at the age of seventeen, one year out of school. All through secondary school—the big convent, as they called it locally, she worked a milk-round with her father, setting out in the van in the dark to collect the milk from the bottling plant, working through the dawn running between van and doorsteps, back doors, side doors, front gates, farm gates, carrying her half of the crate at the seven shops on their route, jumping off at nine to go to her lessons in the convent and leaving her father to finish the round on his own. At Creevy Court Major Coleman's housekeeper Madge always had two pints of milk a day and half a pint of cream on Saturday.

She worked the year between school and marriage in a newsagent's shop in Nenagh, driving there and back on a motor scooter she had bought with her milk-round money. Her father called it the chicken-chaser. Her father farmed sixty arable acres when his milk round was done. Noeleen learnt to drive as soon as her feet reached the tractor pedals and when she was fourteen she won Queen of the Plough at the Nenagh ploughing match.

Her father did not take to Eddie O'Keefe. He offered the younger man the milk round as a kind of a dowry and as a test to see was he anything more than just a charmer.

'That's slave labour,' Eddie said when told how much he'd make out of four hours' work six mornings a week. Eddie worked at the garage where Noeleen bought the chicken-chaser and he was going to set up on his own. He had a way with engines and was a natural salesman.

Eddie persuaded his widowed mother to sell the farm, which he had never wanted to work, keeping the old farmhouse as her home. He used part of the money to set up two pumps, one petrol, one diesel, outside the hay shed. He dug a pit in the hay shed, put up a tin sign that could be seen from the road, 'Eddie O'Keefe Auto Engineer' and called it his workshop. With the rest of the money he built a new bungalow for his bride a field away from his mother's house.

Noeleen had her first child, Mark, shortly before her eighteenth birthday. Helen, named for Noeleen's mother, followed when she was twenty, then Jacintha and Damien. She had no babies for four years, then Conal came along and within another two years, at the age of twenty-eight, her last baby, Lucette, was born.

The auto-engineering business went well for Eddie O'Keefe. He bought back one of the roadside fields, poured tarmac over it and hung flags and bunting along the front under a sign saying 'Eddie O'Keefe Auto Engineer – Car and Tractor Sales'. He drove a series of Mercedes himself, having always been an admirer of German mechanics, and Noeleen had the use of a succession of slow-sellers from the used-car lot, often Skodas or Ladas, to chauffeur the kids around in.

She took the part-time job in Barry's the year that Mark left school and Lucette reached her fifth birthday. She had to pay part of her wages to Jacinta or Damien to mind the little ones, but she did not work for the money, even though she enjoyed having something of her own to spend. She worked for the change of scene and the company—to get out of the house and to have a bit of a laugh. Eddie was devoted to his business, and apart from an occasional visit to a roadhouse after a ploughing match or a point-to-point, never thought of taking Noeleen out. Their courting days were over, he said firmly whenever she brought the matter up.

When Noeleen found, as she often did, matches or receipts from fancy restaurants in Limerick—The Jasmine Garden, De La Fontaine—Eddie explained them away as business entertaining. She had suspected for years that he was unfaithful to her—ever since she found a pair of red lace underpants in the back seat of the Merc on her way home from hospital after having Lucette. Nowadays they had sex only rarely—usually when she came home a little squiffy after accepting too many drinks from her customers in the bar. Then she made the first move; Eddie never made the first move anymore. Noeleen took this sadly as proof of the existence of a girlfriend or girlfriends, but never challenged him on the matter. What good would come of rocking the boat?

When Helen reached her eighteenth birthday, she got part-time work in the bar too, to help her to pay her way through college. Helen was doing a degree in Business Studies in Limerick. Noeleen enjoyed the job even more once she had Helen there. Helen was as fond as her mother of a bit of a laugh. They were both wiry dark-haired women of middle height, dressed in jeans and cheerful checked shirts, and were often mistaken for sisters.

On the nights that his women were out working, it was Eddie O'Keefe's habit to drop into the bar about half an hour before closing time and have a couple of jars. That was how he had first met Elaine Fahy. It was a week after Noeleen had started her job at Creevy Court. She was to work part-time from April to October and if she and Elaine found it too much in July and August, then Helen would put in a few hours too. Elaine intended to close from November to March, and said she could do with only two hours a week for those months. Creevy Court was not a big house; she would have room for a maximum of twelve guests a night in the six bedrooms.

'We'll manage that, no bother,' said Noeleen. She was looking forward to seeing some new faces around the place.

'If it goes well, maybe the following year I'll start doing dinner. I could do a course at a cookery school in the winter.' She was thinking of Paris.

'They say you can't go wrong with the cookery school over at Ballymaloe. Kay who's married to Billy who owns Clancy's Pub in Nenagh, did the bar food course and she's been flying it ever since with the carvery lunch.'

They were talking over the bar at Barry's. Elaine had decided to go down to the pub since it was Noeleen's night. She was not usually a pub person, but it seemed the best way of meeting her neighbours. She had gone to Mass the first three Sundays in order to show herself and quell the curiosity which attended her every appearance in the local shops, but had spoken to no one. For weeks after that she had been taken up with the work on the house. This was her first visit to Barry's, Tarrantstown's only pub.

The half-dozen drinkers in the lounge fell silent as she came in. Noeleen called her over and introduced her around as Elaine Fahy, daughter of Hanora Fahy, now the new owner of Creevy Court.

'Wasn't I at school with your mother?' said a wizened man with a nutcracker chin sitting next to a Zimmer frame. 'Fine girl Nora was too. Then off with her to England and never another peep out of her.'

'She died three years ago,' said Elaine. 'The big C.'

'God rest her soul,' said Noeleen. 'If she was at school with Mickey Hogan she must have been a fair old age. What age are you, now, Mickey?'

'Eighty-seven.'

Elaine was on her third gin and tonic when Eddie joined her at the bar. Her first impression surprised her. He was slim but not tall, maybe 5'8 to her 5'4. He did not look like a father of six and he did not look like a Tipperary *garagiste*. She had assumed someone brasher. His dark green Barbour jacket was frayed at the cuffs and shiny from use. Under it he wore a soft check shirt in brown and yellow; a red wool scarf was thrown over the outside of his coat. He took scarf and coat off as one and she saw he was wearing dark green plus fours with matching socks.

'I killed a brace of pheasant this afternoon over Kilcaw way; they're still in the back of the car. We've a freezer full of birds already. Would you like them?'

'I'd love them! I've a friend from London coming over at the weekend. Why don't you and Noeleen join us for dinner on Saturday night?'

She listened with astonishment to what she was saying.

But, then, why not ask the help to dinner? How had she got so grand, so *English*? Noeleen wasn't just help, she was her friend. Noeleen and Eddie were nice people. They were going to be very useful to her, she could tell that straightaway. They were also the only people in Tarrantstown she knew.

'We'd be happy to, wouldn't we Noeleen? Helen can cover for you here. It's time you had a night out.'

'Who's the London friend Elaine?' said Noeleen. 'An old flame?'

'No such luck, he's just a pal.'

Elaine was a fit, small-boned woman, and very sporty. She restored the tennis court and gave a couple of afternoon tennis parties with the help of Doctor Walsh and his wife, Patricia, both keen players. That first summer, in spite of the demands of her bed and breakfast business, she bought a sailboard and a wetsuit and spent many early afternoons out on the lake. Her first local lover was her boardsailing instructor, Declan Dermody. Their usual rendez-vous was Creevy Court's boathouse, to which she had added a daybed in the course of her redecoration. He was almost twenty years her junior. When he left in October for a job in Lanzarote, she wished him well. After two husbands in ten years, Elaine was not looking for long-term complications.

In the autumn Elaine took up shooting. She went out after woodcock with Eddie, Noeleen and Mark on the first of November and was so taken with the sport that she went into Limerick the very next day to a gunsmith recommended by Eddie and bought herself a Webley & Scott. She was considering getting a dog too, but Eddie and Noeleen insisted she could use one of their three setters any time she liked: 'We've more than enough dogs for one family. Why go making work for yourself?'

On Christmas day Elaine cooked dinner for the whole O'Keefe family, including Eddie's elderly mother. It was a way of thanking the O'Keefes, and especially Noeleen, for all the help they had given her in her first season. It would be a treat for Noeleen because although she kept a well-run house, she had never learnt to cook anything beyond soda bread, a roast dinner and the basic fry. These days Mark made the evening meal—the tea—with Helen sharing the chores when she was home from college. Noeleen marvelled at the children's exotic taste in food: 'Chicken curry he gave us last night, and the day before that it was avocado and pasta that they learnt from the television.'

Elaine put a set of coloured fairy lights up around the porch and Mark helped her string white and silver lights on a tall tree in Creevy Court's front hall. She had not asked her London friend back for a second visit, preferring the easy company of her new neighbours.

The party really began after they had all eaten. Elaine invited several of her acquaintances to drop over in the early evening— the tennis-playing Walshs, the Barrys from the pub, and an American couple who ran an even fancier B&B than hers a few miles up the lakeshore. In true festive spirit, she even invited Declan Dermody, who was home for a few days. Helen brought her guitar along and there was a sing-song. All the O'Keefes had strong voices. Noeleen sang "Summertime" with her eyes shut; she sang with such strength of feeling that Helen reduced her guitar accompaniment to a whisper. Her husband sang *Me and Bobbie Magee* in a rich baritone, and they all joined in the chorus: 'Freedom's just another word for nothing left to lose . . .'

The singer looked straight at Elaine as he sang and she looked straight back at him.

Soon after Christmas, Noeleen started to suspect that her erring husband was involved with somebody new, somebody more important to him than the others. Dunhill aftershave appeared in the bathroom. He changed from white Y-fronts to blue and white striped boxer shorts. He gave all his socks bar the shooting socks to the Saint Vincent de Paul and bought new ones in matte gray silk. Then he bought a leather suitcase.

'There's a motor show in Leeds. I'm looking for a new tractor dealership. Romanian. What'll I bring you back?'

The mistress of Creevy Court was away too, but it never occurred to Noeleen to link the two. Elaine, she happened to know because she had just got a postcard, was skiing in the French Alps. Elaine went skiing every year at this time, she told Noeleen. The snow and the sun, the *glühwein* and the nightlife . . . It seemed to Noeleen, who had never liked snow, a long way to go and a high price to pay for a drop of wine and some nightlife. Mark had been at school with Declan Dermody, and Noeleen knew what had been going on in the boathouse the previous summer. She was more envious than shocked.

What Noeleen didn't know was that Elaine intended to take a break in London on her way back from skiing, and Eddie was heading off to meet her. There was a motor show in Leeds; he had been careful about his alibi because the kids were so smart, but he had no intention of going anywhere near it.

While Eddie was away and Helen was back at college, Noeleen let herself be driven home by Dessie Hogan, the captain of Barry's darts team. Dessie Hogan was the sort of man who automatically made a pass if he found himself alone with a woman. Noeleen knew this when she accepted the lift.

Noeleen did not let him in the house where her small children were sleeping, but she let him have her up against the side of his ancient Toyota. It was the first time she had been unfaithful to Eddie. She was surprised to find that she felt better, not worse after. She had a moment of anxiety that Sunday as she approached the Communion rail, but nothing happened so she reckoned that God, whom she secretly doubted anyway, either didn't exist or didn't mind. Noeleen had got away with it.

She did not intend to stick with Dessie Hogan. There were younger men on the darts team with better cars and more staying power. It was a good laugh; all she missed was someone to share it with. Maybe Elaine, when she got back.

Elaine Fahy never intended to have more than a little fling with Eddie. It was a long quiet winter, and she needed a distraction. She enjoyed showing him off to her London friends, but saw no reason to explain that he was married. 'A neighbour that I go shooting with,' was her usual introduction. All went well in London. It was more difficult when she got back. Tarrantstown was simply too small to be having an affair with a married man, let alone the husband of her friend, but somehow they never got around to calling it off.

Eddie O'Keefe had numerous legitimate reasons for being on her land or in her house; the three of them were, after all, the best of friends. She borrowed their dog Patch; they went clay-pigeon shooting together at weekends, a sport for which Noeleen had a natural gift. She nearly always had the highest score. Some weekends they would drive to the point-to-point together, either in the O'Keefes Merc or in the four-wheel drive that Elaine had recently bought from him, bringing as many children and dogs as they could fit and a cardboard box packed with sandwiches, cake and thermos flasks of tea. Elaine was surprised at how much she enjoyed the O'Keefes' way of life.

And yet, whatever the hour of day or night, wherever she and Eddie were alone, they had to have each other: in his car, his office, her kitchen, her shrubbery, the Kilcaw woods with their guns and dogs, the front porch, even, on rare occasions, in her bedroom. She was often the one who made the first move; one glimpse of him from behind, one casual comment from that deep voice was enough.

The season had already started, but there were no guests in the house. It was eleven in the morning. He had dropped by to return a video Noeleen had borrowed the night before, and stopped for a cup of coffee. They left their coffee mugs on the kitchen table and ran up to her bedroom, pulling each other's clothes off as they went.

Noeleen walked in the open back door, saw the two mugs on the table, followed the trail of clothes, recognised the blue and white striped boxer shorts and stopped in front of the closed door.

She knew, she could hear, but could not believe what was happening inside. To the very last minute she hoped it was some mistake, not her husband and her friend. She listened for another few seconds through the door, and ran back downstairs, knowing the worst. Elaine and Eddie heard the back door slam, and both remembered at the same time what they had both previously forgotten. Noeleen was coming in at eleven to clean the silver.

Noeleen explained the broken arm by saying she had tripped and fallen on the stairs at Creevy Court. It also gave her the excuse for giving up her day job. Only Eddie knew the truth. He had accidentally broken her arm while trying to free himself from her grasp when she flung herself on him in his office. She was waiting there for him when he came back from Creevy Court. She was seeing double in her fury, but had just enough control not to have it out with him in their own house, with the young ones home on their Easter break.

They gave her a sedative at the hospital, mistaking her uncontrollable weeping for another kind of shock. Eddie waited on a hard bench in Accident and Emergency for three hours, thinking things over. He decided to stop seeing Elaine and go back to his family; he was regretting that he had ever got involved with her. Previously he had followed a simple rule: never fool around on your own doorstep. Only do it in Limerick or Dublin or London, anonymous big city stuff with women of the world, who were happy to screw him in return for a good time. Elaine had always been a kind of madness. He should have known when to stop. He would ask Noeleen to forgive him, and promise not to be unfaithful to her again. Noeleen had always been a good wife to him. They would be a happy family once again and he would have no more to do with Elaine.

Her arm had mended nicely by the time he found out about the darts team. He had not seen Elaine since the day of the silverware, and had given her no explanation for his sudden disappearance. He noticed her in the distance on several occasions, looking after him, staring his way, and could not work out if her stares were meant to express longing or reproach. They finally came face-to-face one fine June afternoon on the main street of Nenagh.

'I think you owe me an explanation,' she said, standing in his path.

'I thought it was obvious. I've gone back to my wife. It's over. I didn't think you were sentimental.'

'You don't know about the darts team, do you?'

'What about the darts team?'

'Ask Noeleen. Or ask the darts team. The husband is always the last to know.'

She gave him a condescending smile, turned her back, and walked towards her car.

Eddie came into the house, every fibre in his body trembling with rage. Lucette was sitting at the kitchen table doing her maths homework. Conal sat opposite her, spreading blackcurrant jam on to a slice of thickly buttered soda bread.

'Where's your mother?'

Conal shrugged and Lucette shook her head. Eddie's fist came down on the table.

'Answer me when I ask you a fucking question. Where's your mother?'

His roar brought Noeleen in from the front room where she had been ironing while watching an old video of *Dallas*. She shooed the two children out the back door.

'I won't have that language in front of the children. Are you out of your mind?'

He lifted his right hand and hit her hard on the left ear. As she reeled to the right he caught her a blow on the other ear. Through the ringing noises she heard the words 'darts team'. He hit her again and again but she made no sound. Whatever else, she did not want the children to know what was going on.

When Eddie had driven off, Conal and Lucette crept back in to find their mother sitting at the kitchen table, her head in her hands.

'I've a terrible headache. Will you fetch me some aspirin and I'm off to bed,' she whispered.

'Where's Daddy gone?'

'Don't worry. He'll be back.'

The deafness came and went. At times words became only sounds and their strangeness alarmed her. But it was not as bad as the constant humming which seemed to happen right in the middle of her head. In the night she often got up and sat on the sofa with the headphones of Conal's personal stereo clamped to her ears, playing any kind of music loudly in order to drown out the humming. She blamed the deafness on an ear infection and used it as an excuse for leaving her job at Barry's. Eddie told her he'd walk out on them if she ever set foot in there again, and she believed him.

The next Saturday she went to confession in the cathedral in Limerick.

'He's a good husband to me, Father. I don't know what got into me. It was a kind of a madness, like. I wasn't myself at all.'

The priest spoke in a consoling tone of voice, but she could not make out his exact words. She could not hear the penance either, so she knelt and said fifteen decades of the rosary, just to be sure she had it covered.

She had to tell Helen about Eddie and Elaine because she could not bear Helen to take a summer job at Creevy Court again.

'We've known that ever since you broke your arm, mother,' said Helen who usually called her mother Noeleen. 'One minute you're in and out of each other's houses like she's family, and the next minute it's like she doesn't exist any more. We're not stupid around here.'

'Even the little ones?'

'Lucette said you should get a divorce but I told her she's been watching too much *Dallas*. We don't have divorce here.'

'Your father's a good man. Try not to hold it against him.'

'Maybe you should see somebody. You know there's a pattern it follows. Women who stay in violent marriages must be taught to get out of them, to break the pattern. I was reading about it in a magazine the other day.'

'You young ones know everything nowadays. It's not so simple; it's never that simple. I am not in a violent marriage, we've just been through a bit of a rough patch that's all. We were grand before Elaine Fahy came along, we were grand. And in future you can mind your own bloody business, you and your magazines. You don't know everything!'

Noeleen ran out of the kitchen and locked herself into the bathroom where she ran the taps to hide her sobs.

'Where have you been? It's three in the morning. It's the second time this week you haven't got home until three. Where have you been?'

'It's none of your business where I've been.'

'You've been with that bitch again, haven't you? I can smell her on you.'

'So what if I have?'

'You might at least have the decency to deny it.'

'Decency? You're talking to me about decency? I'll show you decency, you whore.'

The ears again. This time she screamed loudly and jumped out of the bed. She hit back at him, cutting his temple with the heel of his own shoe. Then she ran into the sitting room. She could hear Mark and Damien and Helen and Jacinta shouting at their father and Eddie shouting back. Then the back door slammed and she heard his car engine start up.

'It's not true, Mammy, is it? What he said about the darts team, it's not true?'

'Not Dessie Hogan, Mother. Tell me he's lying.'

'Say something Mammy.'

Noeleen took to her bed and stayed there for five days. The children were in and out of the bedroom packing their father's things into black bin liners and the leather suitcase. They decided that if their mother had made an unfortunate mistake, it was because their father had driven her to it. How could their mother compete with a rich stuck-up bitch like Elaine Fahy? It wasn't fair. If that was what he wanted, let him have it. They carried the bin bags and the suitcase over to his office and left them outside the door.

'Stay as long as you like,' said Elaine. 'Make yourself at home, if you haven't already.'

'I didn't mean it to end up like this. To be thrown out by your wife is one thing, but to be thrown out by your own children . . .'

'Poor Eddie. Nobody appreciates you but me. Have another drink.'

Life at Creevy Court in the cold December days was very comfortable, but he missed his children, especially the little ones. He missed his dogs, and in an odd sort of a way he missed his wife. Elaine was great, but he was not the man to eat caviar every day.

'Let's go out somewhere,' she said, one evening. 'Let's drive over to The Grange for a meal.'

'What for?'

'No particular reason. To cheer ourselves up? Because I feel like it?'

'I'd rather stay in by the fire. There's a match on later I wouldn't mind watching.'

'Do you know what they call her in the village, Mammy? They call her "the scarlet woman". Mrs. Keane won't serve her in the shop and Doctor Walsh never asked her to his Christmas drinks.'

Even so, Elaine Fahy had her man and Noeleen had no one. Her children were like a self-contained unit; they didn't need her any more. The older ones would look after the younger ones. They would always have a home.

She was not able for much in any case. Mark and Helen were organising the Christmas dinner. Eddie had arranged a banker's order for their support without even being asked, and had doubled it for the Christmas. Noeleen didn't have the heart for the usual Christmas shopping trip to Limerick. It reminded her of the sadness she felt, alone with her father, on the first Christmas after her mother's sudden death on St. Stephen's Day. She gave Helen what was left of her bar money and asked her to get presents for everyone from her. Lucette and Jacinta helped to wrap them while the boys put up decorations. When Helen brought out her guitar for Christmas evening carols round the tree with Mrs. O'Keefe, Noeleen went to bed with Conal's stereo.

She refused to go to Mass on Christmas morning, but for the children's sake, for the sake of the children, and for Eddie's mother whose wits were now wandering, she sat through Christmas dinner. Before they ate, she watched while they opened their presents and then she opened hers. The two eldest had bought her a portable cassette player of her own with a radio and headphones. The others had given her tapes of her favourite singers. Presents always made her sad, but this seemed the saddest of them all, the start of the rest of her life as a lonely, abandoned wife. Before they had always given her pretty, feminine things—perfume, eye shadow, sweaters and scarves; now they were trying to make up for Eddie not being there.

The phone rang at two-thirty, just as they were sitting down to eat. Helen answered. Nobody wanted to speak to Eddie until Noeleen stood up. It was her birthday as well as Christmas Day, and she felt that meant she should make the first move. She pulled the phone lead around the other side of the kitchen door the way the children always did when they did not want their conversation to be overheard.

'How are ya?'

'Happy birthday.'

'Would you like to drop by later for a drink. Say hallo to the children?'

'I get the impression they don't want to see me.'

'They'll get over it. I'll have a word with them.'

'Maybe another time. We have some people coming over later and I said I'd give a hand.'

'I'm talking about your own family on Christmas Day and you talk about *people coming over.*'

'Noeleen, calm down . . .'

Through her angry sobs he heard somebody put the receiver down on a table, and say soothing words. Helen he thought; then he was cut off.

Mark took her in to the sitting room and settled her in an armchair by the fire with a glass of port. They had to cut eighteen inches off the bottom of the tree to fit it into the bungalow, and even so the star at its tip touched the ceiling, as if it were holding it up. Noeleen remembered the previous Christmas with Elaine, her tree decorated only with silver and white, standing ten feet tall in the entrance hall of Creevy Court.

It came to her all of a sudden: she had not fought hard enough for Eddie. He had no idea how much she wanted him back, wanted to be a whole family again instead of an invalid or a kind of half-wit amidst all these brave sensible children. She wanted Eddie back at home by her side where he belonged.

She waited until the others had finished their meal and left the kitchen. Then she rang Creevy Court. She spoke in a hissing whisper so that the children in the front room would not hear.

'I want him here. Do you hear me, you bitch? Send my husband home. Tell him come back where he belongs, or you'll be sorry.'

Eddie came on the line.

'Noeleen, calm down. Why this fuss all of a sudden? Go back to the children and don't be causing trouble.'

'Tell the bitch I'll fucking kill her if she doesn't let you come home.'

'Stop that foolish talk right now. Get me Helen or Mark. You need help.'

'Fucking bastard!' she whispered. 'You'll get what's coming.'

She hung up then. It was the first time she'd ever used the word "fucking", and it gave her a special thrill. She felt so much better that she was able to join the children in front of the television in the front room, and sip another glass of port.

As dusk was falling, she said she needed some fresh air. She walked down to the phone box with change in her pocket and dialled Creevy Court.

'Hallo?' Elaine sounded nervous.

'Send him home or I'll fucking kill you.'

'I'm going to complain to the gardaí. It's illegal to make threats like that. You'll be sorry.'

'Send my husband home or I'll kill you. I don't want to have to do it, but if it's the only way to get him back, then I fucking well will.'

She hung up and went home to wait until the children had gone to sleep.

Elaine and Eddie decided not to call the guards.

'It's probably just a kind of Christmas blues,' said Elaine. 'I know what it's like. I've been through it twice myself.'

'Even so, I'd sleep easier if we had your gun in the bedroom with us.'

'My gun in the bedroom! You've got to be joking. Noeleen is too sensible . . .'

The children and their solicitor did everything in their power to have Elaine Fahy charged with manslaughter, preferably murder. The Director of Public Prosecutions ruled that there was no case to answer. She had fired in self-defence under extreme provocation.

The Scarlet Woman was now referred to in the village as 'the murderess'. Elaine was in deep shock for weeks, and for a long time afterwards she suffered from short-term memory loss. She regularly lost track of her handbag and her car keys. She did not know which bills she had paid, and which were still owing. She could not go out on her own because she was afraid of what strangers might say to her. She needed Eddie to look after her.

Eddie's tractor and car trade dried up overnight. His children would not talk to him. Creevy Court was put up for sale, while Elaine and Eddie looked for a similar guesthouse in another part of the country. They had no option but to stay together. The shooting incident had bound them together more firmly and irreversibly than any marriage vows.

An Explanation of the Tides

THE HERRING FLEET was in the harbour. Three Polish factory ships were moored up the river near the new bridge. Every evening small trawlers that had been at sea since dawn steamed in past Raffeen, each with a flock of gulls screaming in their wake, to sell their catch to the Poles. You could smell the herring half a mile inland; in the town itself the greasy stench was overpowering. Herring could be bought on the quay for a couple of pounds a box, but with the reek of fish guts in the air day and night, no one could face eating the damn things.

It was early autumn, the season of equinoctial gales. The tourists had at last left town, and we were on our own in The Boatman, the usual crowd, thrown together by the arbitrary fact that this was the only bar in Raffeen.

Nobody travelled the two miles from town to go to The Boatman once the summer was over. In good weather you could take your drink outside on to the sea wall and warm yourself in the sun, watching the tides come and go. Peadar Bligh, the owner of The Boatman did not believe in central heating, and in winter the place was uncomfortably cold.

Every evening at four o'clock on the dot, after his mug of tea, Peadar came into the bar and lit a small coal fire on the far side of the room. Old Jack, the Tide Inspector, and any of their pensioner friends who happened by had priority in front of it. The Tide Inspector, when he was not hogging Peadar's miserable little fire, would be found leaning on the harbour wall, inspecting the tide. 'It's in!' he would shout as you walked by, or 'It's out!', depending. Life was never dull in Raffeen.

I like to stand at the bar myself, or sit at it on a tall stool if I'm in for a long session. On this particular afternoon I was sitting.

I am by nature idle, and perhaps the greatest and most satisfying form of idleness is to be sitting on a tall stool inside the window of a bar, preferably a waterside bar, in mid-afternoon on a sunny day. It is not the same on a rainy day. The decision to go daytime drinking when the rain is pouring down has a certain logic, which it lacks in sunny weather. The sunlight filtering through the motes that gather by the window adds an extra dimension to the decision to sit indoors, sipping pints. I was particularly fond of the light in Peadar's bar, which was reflected off the sea on the other side of the harbour wall. It was at its most golden on autumn afternoons, reaching a crescendo at around seven, after which the sun sank slowly behind the town at the western end of the bay.

'Any sign of Jeff? Anyone on for a few hands of poker? Ten pence in and half the pot maximum bet?'

It was Charles, looking for a poker game. What drinking is to me, gambling is to Charles. Jeff, an amiable character from Maine who lived with Maria and spent most days building dry stone walls, had not been in. I was not inclined to play myself, being as usual broke, and neither was Maria the bar person (never, never call her a barmaid), being broke also. Charles went out without ordering a drink.

I was staring at my pint when Maria interrupted my reverie: 'Thomas? Thomas?'

'What?'

'There's a man works down the chip shop thinks he's Elvis.'

A remark of characteristic banality. I did not consider it worth replying. My silence provoked her. I enjoy that.

'At least he's alive. I'm not so sure about you.'

I ignored her as usual, having heard the song from which these words were taken on the tinny little radio behind the bar only half an hour back. She retired to her stool at the opposite end of the bar, and started to read a magazine.

Linda, who often spent the afternoon in Peadar's drinking tea, a most despicable thing to do in a pub, ordered another mug. That kept Maria busy for a full five minutes, watching the kettle while she waited for it to boil. Meanwhile Linda picked up the magazine that Maria had put down.

'I don't believe it,' she said. 'It's disgusting,' She started giggling. Linda has a rather attractive laugh, probably the best thing about her.

'What's disgusting?' I asked.

'My God! He's alive!'

You can guess who said that.

'Sarah Miles drinks her own piss.'

'What?'

Linda read a quote from the actress, putting on what she thought was a posh English accent: 'Most people, I know, would find it utterly repulsive. We are taught to regard urine as waste, as something not nice. But when it first comes out of your body [pause here for more giggling] it is completely sterile. It doesn't actually taste awful at all . . .'

Peadar Bligh, alias Big Ears, heard the laughter from his sitting room overhead and came scuttling downstairs with a mug of tea in his hand. It was nearly fire-lighting time.

'What's this?'

'Sarah Miles. Drinks her own piss.'

'Go on!'

'It's true. Look. Urine Therapy. Read it.'

Peadar read slowly, his finger crossing the page beneath each word as he declaimed slowly, in a tone of disbelief:

'Urine Therapy. It cannot do any harm. Urine is sterile when it leaves the body but quickly decomposes, so it should be drunk immediately. In a healthy condition, it won't smell nasty and will taste of whatever you have recently been eating or drinking . . .'

That was enough. Peadar put the paper down and laughed

uneasily. 'Is that a fact?'

'Sarah Miles always was crazy,' I told them. 'I met her once at an opening night when she was married to Robert Bolt.'

'I'm not going to try it,' said Maria.

'What aren't you going to try?' said Jeff, who had just come into the bar with Charles. Peadar gave him the magazine.

'That's disgusting,' said Charles.

'That's what I said,' said Peadar.

'Drinking your own piss?' Jeff had the sort of voice that carries effortlessly across three fields, and a pleasant New England accent. 'I wouldn't drink my own piss if I was dying.'

'How do you know?' Maria was always good for an argument.

'Sarah Miles is bats,' said Charles.

'That's what I said.'

'Have you told Charles about the man in the chip shop yet?' asked Linda, smiling at Charles. All the women liked to flirt with Charles. What is it about gamblers?

Linda, Maria, Jeff, Charles and even Peadar were being extremely silly and very noisy. My pint was empty and neither Peadar nor Maria noticed. I had to knock my empty glass on the counter and call 'Pint' five times before Peadar reacted.

'Pint of Sarah?' he asked with a nasty look in his eyes.

As he started pulling the stout, a small dog hurled itself against the glass panes of the front door. The door rattled noisily on its catch, and the dog threw itself at the glass again.

'Here comes Scottie and his wee doggie!' said Jeff.

'I'm not having that dog in here,' said Peadar putting a head on my pint. 'He's crawling with fleas.'

Peadar said the same thing every afternoon at this time. Scottie's dog—known only as 'wee doggie'—was indeed a flea-ridden little creature, but Scottie himself was not all bad. 'Ye cannae shove your granny off a bus' was his motto and theme song. He played a good hand of poker when sober. He had turned up in Raffeen a few years before and stuck, as people tend to.

'Throw it in the tide,' said Jeff. 'Filthy mutt.'

'That's it!' cried Peadar. 'I'll do that if Scottie brings him in here again. I'll throw that dog in the tide.'

Nobody believed him.

A few seconds later Scottie came in, the filthy wire-haired terrier at his heels.

Peadar was on the other side of the bar before Scottie had the door closed, and was giving out in a high-pitched whine:

'I've told you before, I tell you every day, I am not having that animal in my bar, and this time I mean it. Get out! Get out! Get out! Out out out out OUT.'

Before Scottie had time to react Peadar had picked up the short-legged beast by the scruff of its neck and was holding it at arm's length. He marched out of the bar and across the road to the sea wall.

The Tide Inspector, who was leaning on the wall, shouted 'It's in!'

Peadar held the animal out in front of him and dropped it over the wall. Its pathetic howl was silenced by a splash. Calista saw us from her house and came running over. We were all standing at the water's edge, some cheering Peadar, some cheering the dog which was paddling its way around to the slip, a look of pure terror in its eyes.

'Ma poor wee doggie,' Scottie kept repeating. 'Come on fella. Ye'll make it, noo trouble, ach, ma poor wee doggie . . .'

Peadar was waiting at the slip beside Scottie. As the dog passed him, still in deep water, Peadar pushed its head under with his foot.

This was too much for Scottie.

'You right bastard!' he shouted, and his fist flew out in the direction of Peadar's face, landing on his left eye. He then delivered a fine head-butt to the solar plexus, which laid Peadar flat on his back.

'Ye'd droon ma poor wee doggie. Fucking bastard!'

Jeff and I helped Peadar to his feet, and walked him back to the bar. The women and Charles stayed on to confirm that the mangy cur had survived. Scottie was crying, large tears rolling down his face. Maria, Linda and Calista comforted him as he patted the dripping dog, which cowered and whimpered at his feet.

'I'm going back to Glasgie wi' ma poor wee doggie,' was the last thing I heard him say.

The day after the incident with Scottie's dog, we had the first gale of the season. The Boatman's clientele divided between those who loved the drama of a storm—myself, Linda, Charles, Calista—and those who hated it—Peadar, Maria, Jeff, old Jack and the Tide Inspector. Nobody was neutral on this matter.

One of the reasons Maria hated gales was that the front door of the pub faced the prevailing wind, and every time a customer came in or went out, the temperature of the bar, which was never warm at the best of times, went down another few degrees. There was a back door to the pub beyond the toilets, outside which stood a malodorous urinal. If you wanted to stay on Maria's good side, always an advisable policy, on stormy days you came and went through the noisome narrow passage that led to the back door.

Peadar had never married, or perhaps we would have been spared the stink from the supposedly disused urinal and the near-Arctic temperature of the bar itself. He had inherited the bar from his father before him, also a Peadar, and done little to the decor apart from employing a signwriter to replace the lettering 'P. Bligh' over the door with the words 'The Boatman'. This was Peadar's idea of keeping up with the times.

Generally when a publican replaces the family name over the door with something fancy—The Jug of Punch, The Anchor (very popular, that one), the whatever Inn, Arms, or Tavern— it is a warning that the bar itself has gone to hell—red plush upholstery, hunting prints and plastic chandeliers, or at the other extreme, knotty, stripped pine furniture and fake memorabilia bought by the yard from some pub interior decorating service: Smoke Capstan, Players Please, Sweet Afton. Not so in Peadar's case. His Old Capstan sign was an original, with genuine rusty edges. His beauty-board fixtures were so ancient that elderly carpenters went into nostalgic raptures at the sight of them. Nobody could remember when the slippery black leatherette seating had last been renewed. Peadar himself had gone round in the spring with a roll of red plastic tape to cover the holes where the crumbling foam rubber was poking through. That was it. His entire preparations for the tourist season. Oh, admirable Peadar Bligh.

Unlike me, Calista never came into the pub before six o'clock in the evening. In fact on the days she didn't go out to work, she never left her house, whose front door could be seen if you looked left out of the bay window at the front of the Boatman, before six in the evening. If it was still light, she sometimes went for a walk and then came into the pub. Other times she came straight across. She was new to Raffeen, her first winter in the village.

She was always surprised when Charles appeared, just as she was leaving her house. 'What a coincidence!', and she would give him a great smile, eyes as well as teeth. She never suspected he had been spying on her all day, keeping her house under observation, either from his house or from The Boatman's front window, and timing his movements to coincide with hers. He had never been known to go for walks before; now he accompanied Calista on all of hers, and Calista was an all-weather walker. I was not sure about Calista yet. She looked a bit exotic: dark-haired, aloof. Not the usual type to land up in Raffeen.

The evening of the storm they had just walked down the hill together, she in a yellow oilskin jacket, he in a blue one, and were standing directly outside the window of the Boatman, looking over the sea wall. As a wave suddenly surged up, they ran back across the road laughing, and just missed a drenching.

Peadar was pulling down the blind at that moment, and in a reflex action he gave a warning shout through the closed window, which they could not possibly hear. Maria went off duty when Peadar pulled down the blind, but she often stayed for a drink, waiting until Jeff knocked off work. Then Jeff of course wanted a drink, and Maria had another, and so it went on. It was not unusual to find them still in The Boatman at closing time, and even later if Peadar was in the mood.

Charles and Calista came in the front door followed by a cold damp gust of wind.

'It must be blowing a Force Eight out there,' said Calista. 'The sea's a beautiful mess, all churned up.'

'You'll soon get tired of that,' said Peadar.

'It's a very high tide,' said Charles. 'It must be the er . . .'

'You're thinking of equinoctials,' said Calista. 'Equinoctial springs. The highest tide of the year. Full moon in perigee tonight. When the moon is nearest to the earth it's said to be in perigee. The moon's orbit is elliptical as you know.'

'I wish you hadn't told me that,' said Peadar. 'You're worse than the Tide Inspector.'

'Where is he?' asked Charles. 'Surely on a night like this he'd be—'

'He's gone off on a spree,' said Maria. 'Had a couple of large ones at tea time and got the hell out.'

'What happens is that the greatest attraction between earth and moon occurs at perigee, and when this coincides with a new or full moon, full being what we have tonight, the resulting spring tides are greater than average springs, and they are known as equinoctial springs.'

'It's the equinoctial gales that torment me, never mind about the tides. Gales that torment me . . .'

Calista ignored Peadar's moan. She and Charles took their hot whiskeys to a corner table. Charles didn't even ask if anyone wanted a game of poker. He must have got it bad. Linda and Maria on the bar stools to my left were discussing the situation in whispers.

'What do you think will happen when Anna comes home?'

'Stuck-up bitch.'

'But she *is* his wife.'

'He's too good for her. Charles is a sweetheart and all he gets at home is abuse. The things you hear in this job . . . He'd be better off with Calista, that's for sure.'

'Calista says he says he's leaving Anna. Otherwise, she wouldn't have got involved.'

'Well I hope he does, for her sake. I like Calista, and I can't stand Anna. Believe it when I see it though.'

Since it was obvious that I was listening, I made an effort to join in.

'Would you look at those two? Isn't it touching?'

Charles was holding Calista's hands in his on top of the table. At that moment his voice floated up to us:

'The two most important people in the history of the world!'

To which Calista replied, 'Love is both commonplace and miracle.'

Johnny Mathis crooned out from the depths of the crackling radio behind the bar: 'Moon River, wider than a mile . . .'

Maria and Linda sang along softly. The lovebirds held hands and looked deeply into each other's eyes.

'Ladies and Gentlemen *Please!* It's way past time! Have yeze no *homes* to go to?'

There was a freshness in the air next morning as I walked across to The Boatman, but the storm was not over yet. More clouds were massing in the southwest. The air was distinctly different: the storm had at last blown away the smell of herring. I couldn't help feeling cheerful at this release.

'Morning Peadar, Morning Maria.'

Peadar gave me a cross look. 'Your tab has now reached two hundred and fifteen pounds and seventeen pence.'

'You're great at the figures, Peadar. Can we work it up to a nice round sum? Put a limit of three hundred on it? I've a cheque due in the post any day now.'

'Two hundred and fifty.'

'It's a deal.'

'I must be the biggest fool in Munster.'

'Did I ever let you down yet?'

'There's always a first time.'

Maria, who is not all bad, attempted to change the subject: 'I counted seventeen herring boats in today. The harbour's full up. They must've run in from the storm.'

'Most of them could do with a coat of paint,' I said, as Peadar left the bar still muttering. 'Rust buckets. I wouldn't fancy riding out a storm like this on one of them.'

'Me and Jeff had seaweed thrown up on the bedroom windows last night. That's the third floor. I didn't get a wink of sleep.'

'Me neither. Peadar's slates kept crashing. He must have lost a load of them.'

'And the skylight in the gents blew off. Something always goes in the equinoctials.'

'Is that why Peadar gets so nervous?'

'It's the full moon as well as the gales. Haven't you noticed? Every time there's a full moon, Peadar goes a little bit mad. Poor Scottie.'

'Scottie played a good game of poker when he was sober.'

'I expect Charles will miss him.'

'He seems to have other things on his mind at the moment.'

'I think it's lovely—Charles and Calista.'

'It won't last.'

'How do you know?'

'Because he's married. As soon as Anna comes back, it'll all be over. I'll bet you a fiver.'

'But he's in love with Calista. It's obvious.'

'Married men very seldom leave their wives when it comes

down to it. Home comforts have a big pull.'

'Well, you did, Thomas.'

'I did not. She kicked me out.'

'Did I ever tell you about the time I ran aground in Howth harbour?'

'You did, Jack. You did.'

It was later the same day. Peadar came down with his mug of tea, lit the fire, and sat with old Jack, listening to the familiar stories. Eventually Jack's nephew turned up to take the old man home.

'Finish your pint and then we'll go down to the chip shop for our tea.'

Old Jack drank the last of the stout from his glass.

'I can get you a box of herring for a couple of pounds,' he said to Peadar.

'I couldn't look at a herring!' Peadar rolled his eyes.

'It's like the old days,' said Jack, 'When Frankie Kingston and Charlie Hurley had their boat, the *Happy Home*—There's not a herring in the harbour since the *Happy Home* came into Raffeen—they used to say. You'd have been glad of a herring for your tea in those days, Peadar, in all fairness now.'

'How's the form tonight, peteen?' Jack had a soft spot for Maria.

'Grand, Jack, grand.'

'Fair play to you, we might all be dead tomorrow.'

'Ah, Jack . . .'

The nephew stood up and took Jack gently by the arm. 'He's not himself this evening.'

'It must be the equinoctials,' said Peadar. 'I've a touch of it too.'

'Haven't we all?' came a loud voice from the other end of the bar. 'And it's raining in the Gents.' Jeff had come in the back door.

When Peadar pulled down the blind, he and Maria joined

the poker game in the far corner of the bar. Jeff, Charles, Calista and Linda had been playing since six o'clock. Now if I wanted a pint, I had to catch Peadar's attention between hands, or pull it myself. This often happened.

As the one person in the bar not involved in the game, it was only natural that I would pick up the phone when it rang. I recognised the icy tones of Charles's wife Anna. She was apparently so coldhearted that she wouldn't even walk across the road to the pub to let him know she was home, and this after two months away.

'Charles! It's for you!'

The game came to a standstill. Charles listened in silence then said 'Okay' and hung up.

'Sorry. I have to leave.'

'But we haven't finished the hand.'

'Play on without me,' and Charles had gone.

'But he had nearly three quid in the pot!' said Jeff.

'Play on!' roared Peadar, 'He said to play on without him.'

The next day was a Saturday. The storm was over and the sun had a little heat in it. Calista was leaning on the sea wall, and didn't seem to notice me go by. The Tide Inspector was back from his spree. 'It's out,' he said, as I walked past him and into The Boatman for my lunchtime pint.

'Did you see Calista out there?' Maria asked straight away.

'Yes. Has she been there long?'

'Since ten o'clock. Charles was supposed to pick her up at ten and they were going to run away together. I've got her key so that I can feed the cat. She said they might be gone a couple of months.'

Calista stuck her head in the door and looked to left and right.

'Any sign of Charles?'

'No. He hasn't been in all morning.'

'Strange,' said Calista, and went back to the sea wall.

Peadar appeared from above.

'Did I hear Calista?'

'You did,' said Maria. 'Looking for Charles.'

'He's three hours and ten minutes late,' said Peadar.

'When do I get my fiver?' I asked Maria.

'This is going to be hell,' she said.

'Give him a chance,' said Peadar. 'He's got a lot of explaining to do. Anna's a tough nut.'

'I think I see a couple of late tourists,' said Maria.

Two well-built men in blazers and buff-coloured suede shoes came in shortly after. They paused on the threshold, alarmed either at Peadar's lack of home comforts or at the usual low ambient temperature. They were yachtsmen or golfers or possibly both, but not at the moment dressed for sport. Eventually they closed the door and looked at each other, wondering what to order.

I called for a pint.

Jeff and Maria were arguing about Charles's behaviour, Jeff like me, claiming it was totally predictable. I was waiting for a chance to claim my fiver from Maria. Peadar had his hand on the tap to pour my stout when a commanding voice boomed over our heads:

'Two Harvey Wallbangers!'

A hush fell over the bar. Peadar looked up from my pint, his brows low over his eyes, the left one now livid purple and yellow.

'What's that you said?' he asked in a voice that would freeze vodka.

'Two Harvey Wallbangers when you've a minute there.'

Peadar sucked his breath in, turned on his heel and stamped up the stairs to his private quarters. A door banged loudly, muffling an echo of the words Harvey Wallbangers, repeated in the falsetto voice that indicated a major rage in our host.

We sat in silence, staring at our drinks, or in my case, an empty glass, as the tourists shuffled from one foot to the other, occasionally glancing at the ceiling, above which Peadar could be heard pacing like a caged beast and talking to himself. They were shivering, and staring fixedly at the place where Peadar had been standing, as if in a state of shock. Suddenly they rallied, turned around, and scurried as one out of the door and into their little rented car without another word.

Jack's nephew young Jack held the door open and old Jack shuffled in all dressed up in a suit and tie. He'd been 'burying old Miah Harrington' as he put it. A big funeral. As he gave Peadar the details, Calista came in again looking pale and worried.

'I might as well wait here as there,' she said, and ordered a hot whiskey, unheard of behaviour for Calista at this time of day.

'They fired six shots over him and played "The Last Post."'

'What's old Jack on about?' she asked Maria in a whisper.

'A funeral up in Cork.'

'I said to the widow it'll pass. It'll pass, I said.' As Jack spoke loudly to Peadar, Maria and Calista continued their whispered conversation over the bar.

'This is ridiculous. He's over three hours late.'

'Don't worry. He'll turn up.' Maria was trying to sound as if she meant it.

'It'll pass, I said to the widow.'

'I hate this obsession with funerals,' said Maria.

'I've spent the last two hours forcing myself to stay away from the phone. I can't phone him. She might answer.'

'A beautiful burial. Did I tell you they fired six shots over him . . .'

'. . . and they played "The Last Post." You did,' said Peadar. 'About fifteen seconds ago. And you said to the widow "It'll pass". We know all about it now.'

'It was a beautiful burial.'

'I know, Jack, I know!' Peadar swung on his heel and disappeared into the kitchen with the slam of a door.

'Take no notice of him, love,' Maria said to Jack, who was on the point of tears.

'I'd never have been spoken to like that in his father's time, God rest his soul.'

'He's gone very cranky since the storm.'

'Finish your pint now,' said his nephew, 'and we'll move on to where we're welcome.'

'Finish it! I'm only after taking the first sip! Have you no patience, boy?'

This had the makings of an interesting afternoon's drinking.

'Pint!' I called.

'You wouldn't give him a ring for me, would you? I just *can't*.' Calista was pleading with Maria. Calista the aloof who never asked anyone for anything.

'Give who a ring?' Jeff had just come in.

'Jeff! You can phone Charles! Ask him over for a game of poker . . .'

Jeff held his hands out in front of him, palms upwards as if he was pushing something heavy away. 'Oh, no, never get involved, that's my motto. Above all, avoid taking sides in lovers' tiffs.'

'Look! He left his coat here last night. Someone should phone him up and tell him he's left his coat! Maria, please?'

'A beautiful burial, don't you think so?'

'Aye,' said the nephew. 'A beautiful burial.'

'I'd keep out of it if I were you,' said Jeff.

'Thomas! You ring him up and tell him he's left his coat, and would he please come and get it. Would you, Thomas? Please?'

I cannot stand the sight of suffering, and I might well have been persuaded, only Peadar came into the bar at that moment carrying a letter.

'Your boyfriend left that in my letterbox,' he said, handing it to Calista.

The bar fell silent as she tore open the envelope and read the note scribbled on one side of the paper. There was no need to ask what was in it, because she immediately let out a howl:

'How could he do this to me?'

'The age-old cry of the wounded female,' said Jeff into my ear. 'For someone who's supposed to be so clever, she's very naive.'

Maria ran to our side of the bar and put her arm around Calista, but Calista shook her off. Tears rolled down her face as they had rolled two days earlier down Scottie's.

'I think I'd rather be alone,' she said, and she walked out to the sea wall.

'It's the equinoctials,' said Peadar. 'I blame the equinoctials.'

'I blame Charles,' said Maria. 'What a two-faced coward. He led her on. It's unforgivable what he did.'

'Do you think she'll be all right out there?' I asked, struck by a sudden thought.

Peadar peered around the corner of the bay window. 'She's just looking at the tide. She knows all about the tides, didn't she explain the tides to us in minute detail? She'll be all right. In time.'

Later that evening, as I walked home beside the sea wall in the dusk, the Tide Inspector greeted me from the shadows.

'It's out,' he said, nodding wisely.

Star Quality

Izzy Maclaren was early. She drove past the gates and stopped a mile or so down the road beside a slow-flowing stream and got out of the car. It was high summer. An unpaved track crossed the tarred road and forded the stream, as it must have done for hundreds of years. Stunted trees grew beside the stream, and a willow dipped its branches toward the water. In winter the water level must have been twice as high, the flow far stronger. Here on a quiet August afternoon water boatmen hovered over the black surface, legs skittering sideways in the slight breeze, as if pulled by an invisible string. She had not seen one of these creepy, spidery things since her childhood, and she shuddered.

From the corner of her eye she caught a glimpse of bright turquoise that must have been a kingfisher. She was only three or four miles off the main road, but it seemed an immeasurable distance from the everyday world. She had a sudden pang of foreboding, a sense that she was stepping outside normal time, slipping through an existential gap into strange time. She almost panicked and ran.

She had been thinking what a clever location Kurt Karlsson had chosen for his Irish home, hidden away so deeply, yet only about thirty minutes' drive from Shannon Airport. In spite of his Teutonic-sounding name, his mother was a Murphy from County Kerry, and he had come across his house accidentally, on his annual visit to Kerry where he had for many years owned a modest cottage. Karlsson was known primarily for one film: *The Fall of the House of Usher*. 'The world's most handsome man', they called him back in the forties, when he gave such a superb performance as the dying aesthete, Roderick Usher. After retiring from Hollywood to Ireland, Karlsson started to write: he published an enigmatic literary novel, which sold badly but added to his considerable aura. He was rumoured to be working on his memoirs.

He was seen occasionally at Dublin first nights, and at the more important book launches. He always appeared in full stage make-up, great eyes rimmed with kohl, his cheekbones highlighted until they stood out like flying buttresses, lips discreetly reddened, as if waiting for the cameras to roll. According to Izzy's source of information, an antique dealer called Kit, the great actor was bisexual. He had a small group of loyal and very protective friends in the Shannon area who invited him over for cocktails or Sunday lunch. Karlsson only accepted once he had approved the guest list. He preferred very small parties with champagne. The invitations were seldom returned. Izzy had worked hard to persuade her friend Kit to put her case to the great actor. She was on the verge of a breakthrough as an arts journalist, and an interview with the reclusive star would give a great boost to her career.

She did not have much idea of what she was going to talk to him about. She had seen *The Fall of the House of Usher* on television years ago, but was not familiar with his other films, mainly biblical epics, which had a small but fanatic following among the gay community in Dublin. 'He's a great raconteur. Leave it to him,' said Kit. 'He'll charm the socks off you if he takes to you.'

The car felt travel-stale and stuffy after the cool air by the stream. She opened both front windows and drove back to the massive wrought-iron gates. The unmade track across farmland had a line of grass growing strongly along the central ridge. Two large weather-worn stone balls marked the boundary of Karlsson's garden. This was wilder, less manicured than she had expected. Why had she expected a perfectly groomed garden? Because he was Hollywood? It was a semi-wild garden, in impeccably good taste, pale pink climbing roses in bloom against the gray stone house, a cloud of dark pink honeysuckle tumbling over the stable walls.

The drive led to a shady yard, and the back door of the house, which appeared to be the one in use. Its blue paint was flaking off. A large car was parked in the open stables, and a dark green sports car, a Morgan, stood on the gravel outside. She put her bags on the ground and banged loudly with the brass knocker. Not a stir. She walked around the side of the house and looked through the gate, in case he was sitting in the walled garden. She knocked again, and this time she heard distant footsteps. The door opened a few inches.

'Shush! there's somebody asleep upstairs.'

She stretched out her hand and said hallo, at which the door opened a little wider. Kurt Karlsson saw a thin young woman with lank blonde hair, round shoulders drooping apologetically. He thought of an ear of corn on a bad day.

'Hallo, but no thank you. Not today. Oh! Mind the dog, she's got out, Toffee, Toffee . . .'

The great Thespian was barefoot, unshaven, wearing a grubby white T-shirt, white linen trousers hanging on his narrow hips. Even so, he was a striking figure, well over six feet tall, the large brown eyes smouldering, the stubbled chin tilted at a flattering angle.

'Run, run, run! Catch her collar, she doesn't bite. Oh, where are my shoes?'

Toffee was an elderly retriever, and Izzy caught her within a few swift strides and led her back to her distraught owner.

'Thank you. Thank you, she means so much to me, don't you Toffee, you sweetheart? I could never live here alone without the dog. She's a sweet dog. I suppose the least I can do is ask you in for a cup of tea. Kurt Karlsson is my name.'

'I know. I'm Izzy Maclaren. A journalist friend of Kit's. We spoke on the phone, remember? You said you'd be at home on Tuesday afternoon.'

'Oh my God. It's never Tuesday already?'

'Afraid so.'

'I'm so sorry! I thought you were selling something. One gets so careless about time living here. And then I had an unexpected guest arrive last night in a shocking state. Terrible. We stayed up until all hours talking—ah, you've brought me a lemon cake and a bottle of Sancerre. How kind, how thoughtful . . .'

He led her into the cold interior to a formal sitting room with tall windows. He was gone some time. A gray Burmese cat wandered in and lay in the one sunny spot in the room, a corner of the window seat. She heard a kettle boil, cupboard doors banging, plates and spoons rattling.

Dust lay thickly on the carved mahogany side tables and on the marble mantelpiece. Every time she dropped her hand on to the arm of her brocade-covered chair a little puff rose up. Large pictures hung in ornate gilt frames, but it was too dark to make them out. Black-painted boards were covered in threadbare Persian carpets. Izzy was aware that they might be worth a fortune. Then again, they might not.

'Izzy. What's that short for?' He placed a large tea tray on the nearest side table and gave her a dazzling smile.

'Isabel.'

'Then I shall call you Isabel. Nicknames are odious. You actually write under a nickname?'

'It's from when I was an actress. I was told people would remember it for being a bit strange. They'd think twice about Izzy Maclaren, the way they wouldn't about Isabel.'

'Load of tosh, if you don't mind me saying so. Isabel Maclaren has a lovely, dignified ring that is totally absent with Izzy Maclaren. Isabel Maclaren scans perfectly. Izzy Maclaren is an abomination.'

He was charming, there was no other word for it. There was something magnetically attractive about him, the soft American accent, the actorly enunciation, the perfect teeth. She bathed in the glow of his attention, and suddenly had a new understanding of the term 'star quality'. In his presence, everything sparkled.

Kurt picked up a silver teapot and poured tea through a silver strainer.

'It's Earl Grey. Milk or lemon?'

'Neither, thank you.'

'Good girl. My idea of heaven. Lightly brewed Earl Grey and lemon cake. Your lemon cake is little short of divine.'

She smiled at him across the fireplace as if they were in some drawing room comedy.

'How long have you lived here now, Mr Karlsson?'

'Kurt, please call me Kurt, dear girl. I've been here for many, many years now. The farmer I bought it from kept hens in this room, can you believe? See the corner cupboard with the air holes in it? That's where they used to roost. I retained it as a feature.'

'How did you find it?'

'Through a friend. I'm afraid I've let it get terribly run down. I don't have the energy these days, let alone the money, and help is so hard to find. I advertised an apartment over the stables. Rent-free, the use of the car when I didn't need it, and very, very light duties—cleaning, cooking, waiting at table when I entertain, a little gardening, a little chauffeuring—including occasional trips to Dublin all-expenses-paid, staying at the delightful United Arts Club—and a teeny bit of typing, and would you believe, I didn't have one single applicant?'

'Amazing.'

'You wouldn't know anyone? It might suit someone who wanted to live quietly in the country and write. I could offer advice perhaps. I'm useless without a helper. I even lost my cleaning lady. Twelve euros an hour, she was asking, all of a sudden. Did you ever hear the like? Anyway, if you can forgive the relative squalor, I'll take you on the grand tour. If you wouldn't mind leaving your shoes down here, I don't want to wake the sleeping one. Poor darling. She is in the most terrible state, far easier for us all if she sleeps on.'

Beneath the dust the house was indeed beautiful. He had flawless taste. Many of his treasures had been acquired in Italy while filming in Rome. They looked magnificent in this dark Irish interior, their deep reds and golds vibrating in the clear air, the perfect complement to the Irish Georgian furniture. The tour concluded in the garden. In the shrubbery a fine full-length marble Adonis preened on a lichen-clad plinth. A teak bench was placed enticingly against a sunny wall behind a table. Behind the wall there was a hen coop and a fenced-in run.

'Free-range eggs,' said Kurt Karlsson proudly. 'And this is where I grow my salads and my 'erbs. Practically self-sufficient in the summer months.'

As they went back into the hall, a distant clock was striking six. 'Drinkies time,' called Karlsson, echoing the chimes, and he led the way to the kitchen, followed by Toffee and the thin gray cat.

The kitchen, in an extension to the house, was a low-ceilinged room, flooded with sunlight. A red and white check cloth covered a round table, which also held sauce bottles, little heaps of breadcrumbs, and an open jar of marmalade which had attracted a dozen buzzing wasps.

'Be a dear,' he said, nodding towards the drawing room where the tray sat uncollected, the tea crockery unwashed, 'while I deal with these little critters.'

She had just finished drying up as he set two glasses and a bowl of olives on a wicker tray. He handed her a wine cooler containing a bottle of supermarket white from his fridge.

'To the garden.'

They sat on the bench in the evening sun accompanied by the dog Toffee and raised their glasses in a toast.

'Are you working on anything these days? The writing, I mean?'

'Nothing I care to discuss in any detail. I write for my own pleasure and entertainment. Contrary to popular belief, I am not writing my autobiography. I am working on another novel, and have been for some years. I write every morning, religiously.'

'Do you get out much? I mean, who do you see when you go out?'

'The butcher, the baker, the check-out girls at SuperValu, who are my greatest friends. Most of my contemporaries, alas are no longer with us. John Huston was my greatest friend, he introduced me to Ireland. And Gregory Peck would drop by with his lovely wife Veronique. She was a journalist like you, and they met when she interviewed him for a newspaper, isn't that interesting? Peter O'Toole dropped by last week on his way to see Kate. A pity you missed him. And now I have the one upstairs, in a state, but we'd better not go into that. It might lead to scandal. You know what terrible minds people have these days.'

'Won't you tell me who she is?'

'Ever the journalist, one question after another! But where is your tape recorder? Where is your notebook? Perhaps you have an unusually good memory?'

'I'll go and get my tape machine. I hadn't realised we were going to work.'

'I'm only doing this as a favour to Kit, you know. I have nothing to promote at the moment, no reason for wanting publicity. I am living a reclusive retirement, enjoying my solitude. Kit said you were a nice kid, he persuaded me I wanted to help you get on. I thought I'd be interested to meet you. I don't see many young people these days. But if you can't even be bothered to take notes . . .'

'I'll be right back.'

While she was gone Kurt refilled his own glass, drank it, and filled it again. He gave an olive to Toffee who spat it out then stared up adoringly at her master.

'There.'

Izzy put a small tape recorder on the tray between them and helped herself to an olive.

'Do you get up to Dublin much these days?'

'Do you know, I haven't been to Dublin for months. But I did go to London a few weeks ago, for a special screening of *Usher* at the National Film Theatre. I didn't have to say anything, they just wanted the presence, and for that they paid my fare and put me up at a charming little hotel in Basil Street, practically next door to Harrods.'

'I loved that film. You were wonderful in it, just wonderful.'

'Oh my dear, if only you knew how much I regret that film, how it has haunted me ever since. I wanted to turn it down at the time, but they all said to me, Kurt, Kurt, they said, you simply must do it, you are Roderick Usher. It will make you.'

'And didn't it?'

'It made me, and it unmade me. I can truly say I have been haunted by *The Fall of the House of Usher* all my life. The curse of the House of Usher, I usually call it. Nevermore.'

A sudden coldness fell on the early evening air, and Izzy shivered.

'It's getting chilly, isn't it?' said Karlsson. 'Once the sun goes behind that apple tree it's time to move indoors. Can you make an omelette?'

'Um, yes.'

'Then you might as well stay to supper. I'll do the salad. I find that at my age an omelette and a salad and a glass of wine make the ideal supper. You remember where the hens were? You collect the eggs, and I'll pick the salad.'

The omelette was tough at the edges and uncooked in the middle. Kurt sighed as he pushed it around his plate.

'I can see that I'm going to have to give you omelette-making lessons. I learnt from Aldous Huxley's cook in the south of France.'

'Won't you tell me how old you are?'

'Best kept secret in show business. Old enough to have made an omelette for Elizabeth Bowen, if that means anything to you. I wanted to be a writer before I wanted to be an actor. Actor, N.B. I never intended to be a movie star, you know.

I trained as a stage actor. Shakespeare is my first love. I did Shakespeare in summer stock when I was seventeen, and then I did Shakespeare on Broadway. There I was in New York, a writer trying his luck as an actor, a serious student of Shakespeare, but my face was against me. I'm not a leading man, but I look like one, and it was a big disadvantage. I'm really a character actor. I would prefer to play Malvolio, but I was always cast as the Duke Orsino. That, in a nutshell, is the story of my life.'

'I was an actress too once. We must talk about that later. I know exactly what you mean, I hated every minute of it. Oh, I wish I'd brought another bottle of wine. If I'd known you were asking me to supper . . .'

'Open the fridge and look in the door. The corkscrew is over there. Make yourself at home. *Estás en tu casa*, as I used to say to Burton and Liz in Vallarta. But if we have another bottle, you must promise me that you'll stay the night. As you have seen, there's any number of spare bedrooms. I'll put you in the main house for tonight. Just be careful not to wake the sleeping one.'

'Thank you. Thank you so much.'

Izzy had intended to be first down the next morning, to leave a note on the table and run. But someone had got there first. The green sports car had gone, leaving a dry patch on the gravel. There was a large card on the kitchen table covered with a confident italic scrawl: 'Kurt, darling. You saved my life yet again. I'll be back soon. Thank you.' The signature was elaborately ornamented, but Izzy could make it out: Anjelica.

There could only be one Anjelica, with a J. Anjelica Huston. Hadn't he mentioned her father last night? She put a kettle on for coffee and automatically began washing the dishes. Her recollection of the latter part of the previous night was hazy, but she knew that she had asked all the wrong questions. Right now, while she had her coffee, she would make a list of the right questions, and stay long enough to get answers to them. This story could make her name, if she stuck it out.

'Good morning. I see you've taken the initiative. Don't stop because of me. Here's a couple more from Anjelica's room. I joined her for a midnight snack before I went to bed.'

'Kurt, I'm afraid I made a real mess of it last night . . .'

'Think nothing of it my dear. Your omelette-making lessons begin tonight. I will personally demonstrate the famous technique. Meanwhile, it is my habit to spend the morning in the library, working at my writing. You might as well be busy meanwhile. This is where I keep the vacuum cleaner, here are the dusters, and the special beeswax polish. First you dust, then you vacuum, then you polish. Can you remember that?'

'Dust, vacuum, polish. And then I can ask you more questions? For my story?'

'All the questions in the world. I'm not saying I'll answer them, but you can ask me anything you like. And rather than a story, why don't you start work on a novel? I'm sure you've always wanted to write a novel . . .'

Izzy had an unusually bad hangover in which a thick cloud seemed to separate her from the physical world, and deprive her of all will power. She could not even speak, let alone protest.

'When you've finished in here, you can start on the drawing room.'

The voice was cold and formal, as if it belonged to someone else, not the charming man of the night before. 'First you dust, then you vacuum, then you polish. Dust, vacuum, polish. And when you've finished, you can drive me into Limerick and we will go shopping. Jeans, T-Shirts and sneakers for everyday work, and black and white uniform with high-heeled shoes for when we have company. I can just hear my friends now—Kurt! How clever of you! Where did you get her? And I can answer, hand on my heart: all my own invention.'

'Dust, vacuum, polish, dust, vacuum, polish.'

'Good girl! You're learning fast.'

You Can't Call It That

Coleridge hated
Cologne;

I have been to
Cologne, and I hate

Coleridge.

B.S. Johnson

From 'Three Observations'
Penguin Modern Poets, Vol 25, 1975

I'D BETTER SAY straight away that I never knew the late B.S. Johnson, who wrote the story called 'Everyone Knows Somebody Who's Dead'. It's a great title. I really wanted to use it, or rather reuse it, but a loud voice in my head keeps saying YOU CAN'T CALL IT THAT.

I have all his works except *The Unfortunates*, which somebody stole. This is a common complaint among readers of B.S. Johnson. *The Unfortunates* is the one that comes looseleaf in a box, the ultimate experimental novel: read the chapters in whatever order they fall. Somehow this appeals enormously to the sort of people who nick what they think are rare and valuable books, and nearly everybody who once owned a first edition of *The Unfortunates* has had it stolen. I believe I know where mine is, but I am not going to pursue it.

How did it begin, my interest in a little-known writer who killed himself in 1973? Found dead at his home in Islington, Tuesday, 13 November 1973. In the Hispanic world Tuesday the thirteenth has the superstitious connotations that we apply to Friday the thirteenth. November 1973. The time of the wedding of Princess Anne and Captain Mark Phillips and the trial at the Old Bailey of Marian and Dolours Price. It seems like another lifetime.

B.S. Johnson was forty when he died. I was twenty, a reluctant first-year student of English at King's College, London, who, like most first-year students of English, knew nothing about contemporary literature, and had not even heard of her college's recently deceased alumnus.

It must have been about four years later when I first heard his name. I was living in a basement flat in Pimlico, working part-time in a boutique in Knightsbridge while I recovered from three years of Eng. Lit. I needed frivolity. My flatmate was a friend from my year at King's, Liza Black, who had gone straight from college into a trainee job at *Vogue* magazine. Somebody brought Ben Gash to one of our parties. The legendary Ben Gash, reputedly of genius I.Q., who had been two years above us at King's, a remote and much envied figure with long blonde hair who looked more like Brian Jones or the drummer in a rock band than a student (but didn't we all back in the seventies?) and was now doing a PhD at Sussex on one B.S. Johnson.

Of whom, even then, after three years of Eng. Lit. and a B.A. Hons. (English) 2:1, I had never heard.

Ben had a booking at the British Film Institute the next day to view the video of *Fat Man on a Beach*, a TV programme made by B.S. Johnson a few months before his death. This was before videos became everyday objects. It was the first time either of us had actually handled a video, and a woman who worked for the BFI had to show us how to play it. Ben took numerous notes, even though he also had a script, and we watched it over and over again until the woman came back to say it was closing time.

The video was, like much of B.S. Johnson's work, autobiographical, and explained the genesis of his novels and stories. First time through, I couldn't listen to a word he was saying. I was staring in disbelief at a reincarnation. There was this fat man, on a beach, with sandy hair and a snub nose and an amiable, kindly face that could easily turn grumpy, who was the double of my first-ever boyfriend, Robert Warren, who died of leukemia aged nineteen. If Robert had lived to be thirty-nine, he would have looked and talked just like the man I was watching on video. It was eerie.

Ben and I went into the first pub we saw when we were thrown out into the Soho dusk, and drank half pints of bitter and talked and talked and talked about what we had seen. In the last shot of *Fat Man on a Beach*, Johnson is filmed walking into the sea. Ben had heard that, on set, in winter, Johnson had kept going, walking into the cold sea until he was out of his depth, as if wanting to kill himself, and was saved only when he was rescued by a man in the helicopter carrying the camera. I said that sounded apocryphal, the sort of story people make up after a death, and Ben asked me why I thought that, how did I know, and I told him about Robert Warren.

On our next date Ben and I went to the BFI to watch *You're Human Like the Rest of Them*, a black and white short, shot in Super-Eight at a boys' school in Ealing. Johnson was younger here, and looked even more like Robert Warren. It was an exciting piece of work with no words except the words of the title repeated over and over again with more and more urgency until they turned into a kind of primitive drum rhythm—you're human like the rest of them, you're human like the rest of them, you're human like the rest of them . . .

Things were going well with Ben, very well. That summer

I spent the four days a week when I was not working in the boutique, down at Sussex, sleeping with Ben in his single bed in an easygoing shared student house, swimming morning and evening, running hand in hand over the gray cobbles of Brighton beach. It got so serious that I actually introduced him to my parents. My mother cooked roast lamb and made chocolate mousse and Ben wore a corduroy jacket and a roll neck sweater. Suddenly he looked more like an intellectual than a rock drummer.

One day I came home early from work, feverish with a raging headache. I saw clothes scattered in the hall, an empty bottle of champagne, and heard laughter from the sitting room. As I opened the door of my room silently, hoping Liza and her friend hadn't heard me come in, I caught a glimpse of two naked bodies on the sitting room floor. I turned to confirm what I thought my fevered brain had imagined: Ben on top of Liza.

I moved out and he moved in. I went back to college to do an M.A. and lived in a cottage near Manningtree in Suffolk.

Same Story, Another Version

Ben was oddly insecure for someone so attractive. 'You're never going to stay with me, you'll go off with someone else, someone who has money.' 'You care more about your precious Robert Warren, who is dead, than you do about me.' 'You're going to hurt me. I can see it coming.'

Eventually it was as if Ben had been willing it. He was ever more involved in his thesis, spending less and less time with me, while Liza, through her job, was introducing a new crowd to the flat, who were far more fun and far more generous than anybody we had known at King's. We went to opening nights at Covent Garden with journalists on free tickets, and to movies at the Curzon cinema followed by dinner at the Mirabelle with a couple of older men, Americans who were in oil pipeline. And yes, austere weekends eating savoury rice (Ben had turned vegan) in a student house near Sussex University did start to lose their attraction.

I never thought I was the type to hurt anybody, but somehow I managed to hurt Ben. I cannot remember the details at this distance, probably because I was never quite sure what I had done to make us go from being friends and lovers to being deadly enemies—at least on his side.

I have never been hated as strongly as Ben Gash hated me. One-line notes—'Rot in hell, bitch', that kind of thing, appeared in nearly every post. There were abusive phone calls— 'Fucking whore, who are you fucking now?'—and silent phone calls. When friends who had not heard we'd split up asked how I was, he claimed he had never met me. He told one of my tutors at King's that I'd been killed in a car crash. The tutor rang Liza with condolences and I answered the phone. That shook me badly, as intended.

Suddenly the persecution stopped and we heard that Ben had finished his thesis and had taken a job in Eugene, Oregon. The American oilmen cracked open vintage champagne when we told them the news.

One of them in particular was tempting, but I never had the passivity to become a kept woman, which is what Liza eventually became, but that's another story. With the help of the journalists whom I'd met through Liza, I started working as a freelance writer, and within six months I was earning enough to leave the part-time boutique job which I had come to dislike even more than I disliked London University's idea of Eng. Lit. When Liza moved to the bijou apartment in Mayfair that her oil pipeline American was leasing for her, I managed to get hold of a housing association studio flat in Notting Hill.

All of which is telling stories, both versions.

> . . . telling stories is telling lies and I want to tell the truth about me about my experience about my truth about my

truth to reality sitting here writing looking out across
Claremont Square . . .

So do I, but I believe the truth is made clearer if one tells lies.
Even though you shouldn't call fiction that. You can't call it
that. I believe in stories. I love stories.

The truth is I did not go to King's, I went to Queen Mary
College, a less salubrious part of the University of London on
the Mile End Road, dominated by students of geography. Mile
End or Stepney Green Tube. I did get a degree in Eng. Lit., but
I hated my time at QMC so much—for its dullness, its lack of
intellectual stimulation—that a year later I went back to Essex
University, where I had previously spent a year, but where I
could not stay when I got married . . . See how many irrelevant
distractions there are in the truth? It is no help, the so-called
truth.

At Essex I did an M.A. in the Department of Literature, and
met an M.Phil student who sometimes sat in on our seminars.
His name was Paul, not Ben. I'm afraid to give his surname in
case he revives the hate campaign. He was small, very clever
and very intense. He had short dark hair and granny glasses. I
was quite keen on him for a while. I did not introduce him to
my parents, but he took me to Raynes Park to meet his. The bit
about him hating me after we split up is true all right, and it
was frightening.

Liza is part-invention, based on a real flatmate I once had,
crossed with another friend. I did share a basement flat in
Pimlico with someone who had also been to London University
(Westfield College, which, coincidentally is now amalgamated
with QMC) but I can't mention her real name because she did
in fact end up as a kept woman, of a married member of the
aristocracy, not of an American in oil pipeline, hence the hush-
hush. The American did exist, good old Julius, whose name I
can mention because he was divorced and by now he's either
dead or retired to Florida. Julius used to do all his pipeline

business on a telex machine and once told me he always got an erection when a telex came in confirming that he had made various tens of thousands of dollars in the last half hour. Money, said Julius, is the biggest turn-on.

Julius was strictly the flatmate's boyfriend (she two-timed the aristocratic member), although he did occasionally include me in a threesome to the Curzon cinema followed by dinner at the Mirabelle. On Sunday mornings he used to turn up at the flat with armfuls of newspapers and a box of bagels with cream cheese and lox that he'd bought from a Kosher deli on the Mile End Road. Once when I was feeling down about something, he slipped a tenner into my hand and told me to go and buy some flowers for my room, which I did. I liked Julius so much I cloned him in the story so that there was an American in oil pipeline for me too.

See, how distracting the truth is? Paul, the Ben original, really did write a thesis on contemporary literature, including BSJ, but I'm not sure if he ever finished it, and he did emigrate, but not to Eugene, Oregon. I still go cold when I think about how viciously he hated me. He did constantly predict that I would hurt him, 'drop him' we used to say in those days, though I honestly cannot remember how or why we split up. He did take me to the BFI to watch *Fat Man on a Beach* and *You're Human Like the Rest of Them*, and the B.S. Johnson I saw in those films did remind me of a boy I'd had a teenage crush on who died young of cancer, whose name was not Robert Warren, but that will have to do.

More Lies

In my new life as a journalist in Notting Hill I did an odd variety of jobs, from subbing recipes to fine art salesroom reports, but the one I enjoyed most was a monthly round-up of new novels I wrote for an evening paper. I was, however, appalled at the unadventurous, conventional nature of everything I read.

My mind kept going back to the B.S. Johnson novels that

Ben had lent me. I had read them quickly, without making notes. He had of course taken them all back when we split up. All I had left was a photocopy of the final section of Albert Angelo which is called Disintegration, where Johnson attacks the convention of having to speak through an objective correlative, and complains of the utter impossibility of finding 'a paradigm of truth to reality' that could encompass 'the enormity of life'. The photocopy came complete with Ben's notes in the margins: 'Modernism + Realism = Modernist Realism. Any such thing? Yet?' He had also looked up *aposiopesis*, which BSJ uses in the second paragraph and helpfully pencilled a definition in the margin—'[gram.],. Sudden breaking off in the middle of speech."

It is the third paragraph of Disintegration that struck me:

> ---I'm trying to say something not tell a story telling stories is telling lies and I want to tell the truth about me about my experience about my truth about my truth to reality sitting here writing looking out across Claremont Square trying to say something about the writing and nothing being an answer to the loneliness to the lack of loving

> ---look then I'm

> ---again for what is writing if not truth my truth telling truth to experience to my experience and if I start falsifying in telling stories then I move away from the truth of my truth which is not good oh certainly not good by any manner of

In that last line 'not good oh certainly not good by any manner of', suddenly a voice comes alive, if a little posturing, and I see again the fat man on a beach, that earnest, rather worried, expression he used when he was trying to explain something difficult, something that meant a lot to him but was not easy to make clear to other people. Like the way, in the introduction to *Memoirs*, he tells the story of looking for his novel *Trawl* in one of London's biggest booksellers, and finding it on the Angling shelf.

I went to my nearest public library, Kensington. There was no Johnson, B.S. in the catalogue, but they offered to try and find some of his books through inter-library loan.

I mentioned my search to the literary editor for whom I did the new fiction column. Join the London Library, he said. I'll propose you, and find you a seconder.

Ten days later I walked through the tall double doors on St. James's Square and introduced myself to the librarian. I was offered a tour of the stacks, and asked whether I had any particular interest. B.S. Johnson, I said. We looked up his name in the fiction card index and there in careful alphabetical order under the name Johnson, Bryan Stanley William was a list of familiar titles: *Albert Angelo* 1964, *Christie Malry's Own Double Entry* 1973 ed., *The Evacuees* (S.children) 1968, *House Mother Normal* 1971, *Poems* 1964 (l.Eng.Lit), *See the Old Lady Decently* 1975, *Travelling People* 1963, *Trawl* 1966, *Penguin Modern Stories Vol. 7* 1971, *Penguin Modern Poets Vol.25* 1975, with Z. Ghose: *Statement against Corpses* 1964.

No copy of *The Unfortunates*? I asked my guide. She went and had a word with the chief librarian. 'Missing, presumed stolen, I'm afraid, and impossible to replace.'

The more I read, the more I wanted to do something about B.S. Johnson. It was 1983 and the tenth anniversary of his death. Surely I could get a piece published on a dead and unfairly neglected author?

The last straw was a review in the *Sunday Telegraph* of a book with the nauseating title *The Heritage of British Literature*, which had an afterword by Anthony Burgess. The reviewer praises Burgess's witty incisiveness '. . . as when he comments "John Fowles experimented and made money; B.S. Johnson experimented and cut his wrists."'

Something had to be done.

'Why are the English so afraid of experimental writers?' I ranted to my friendly editor, a gentle, elderly Irishman of the old school. 'The French decorate their experimental writers, in Latin America they make them best-sellers, but the English make fun of them, sneer at them even. Are the English scared of experiment?'

'No, my dear, it's not like that at all. Experimental is a term of abuse when applied by the English to writers of fiction. If a work of fiction is perceived to be experimental, then to a certain kind of English reader, to the majority of English readers alas, it has, by definition, failed.'

Thanks to the London Library, I now had copies of six of B.S. Johnson's novels. I owned a copy of *Aren't You Rather Young to be Writing Your Memoirs*, which I had found in a remainder shop near the British Library. But I was still missing *The Unfortunates*, the most experimental one of all, which I had to get my hands on if I were to write a piece defending Johnson's work. Obsessed as I was by the project, I was boring a colleague in the pub with the story of my fruitless search for this particular book.

'You know Stan, don't you?' said my colleague.

'Of course,' I said. Everyone on the paper knew Stan, at least by sight. He was a legendary drunken Irishman of uncertain temper who worked intermittent shifts on the *Diary*, usually wearing a crumpled off-white linen suit. 'What's Stan got to do with it?'

'He was a friend of Bryan Johnson's. I'm sure he has a copy of that book that comes in bits. I remember him mentioning it.'

'*Stan* was a friend of B.S. Johnson?'

It was like being told Frank Harris was a friend of Virginia Woolf. Though on second thoughts, maybe he was.

This Bit is Largely True

I tracked Stan down that very evening in his usual haunt, the French pub.

'Leslie says you're a friend of B.S. Johnson?'

'Was. He's dead you know.'

'I know he's dead. Leslie says you've got a copy of *The Unfortunates*. Can I buy you a drink?'

'A large Grouse. But that doesn't mean I'm going to talk to you.'

'I just wanted to ask you a couple of things about B.S.—'

'Don't call him B.S.! Nobody ever called him B.S.'

'I was going to say B.S. Johnson, only you interrupted.'

'His name was Bryan. That's what his friends always called him. It's only literary groupies like you who pretend they used to know him that call him B.S.'

'But I didn't call him B.S.'

'Oh, go away. You're boring me.'

I suppose it was inevitable after a beginning like that. Within weeks we were talking of marriage. Luckily we never got any further than talking. We parted most amicably and remained close friends. He even let me keep his copy of *The Unfortunates*.

Which was the most terrible disappointment, all about a reporter, the author himself, travelling to a provincial city to cover a Saturday afternoon football match, and being haunted by the memory of a friend who had died of cancer. This is all from memory because when I go to my bookcase to look for the copy of *The Unfortunates* given to me by Stan I find, inevitably, that it is not there.

Stan died suddenly in 1994, aged fifty-one. A few years after an apparently successful operation for lung cancer, he fell and hit his head on a stone step and died a day later of an undiagnosed brain hemorrhage. It would have been neater if the friend who had given me *The Unfortunates*, which was all about a friend who died of cancer, had in fact died of cancer. If I was telling stories, lies, that would be a temptation. But here, in deference to the ideas of B.S. Johnson, I'm telling some kind of truth; though I still maintain that you can't call it that. The truth that matters is the truth that you find in fiction, not the plodding pedestrian true-life story.

Even though Stan was proud of having been a friend of B.S. Johnson, he did not really have much to say about him.

'Why suicide?' I kept asking him.

I couldn't understand, at that age, the depths of pessimism that could drive a person to take their own life.

'He'd separated from his wife, he was missing his children, and he'd got fat. You've read that poem, I presume—"My awkward grossness grows . . ." His wife didn't find him attractive anymore, once he got fat. He was not really gross, but he was a big man. He didn't think anyone would ever want to do it with him again. No more fucking. That's a terrible thought at his age. Forty. So he got into a nice hot bath with a bottle of vodka.'

What impressed Stan most was the way his friend had killed himself.

'In the Roman way.'

After a few drinks, Stan would tell the story over and over again:

'Not like this,'—drawing a line across his wrist as if cutting off his hand. 'Like this,'—drawing a line from his palm up the middle of his arm to his elbow. 'In the Roman way.'

According to the back inside flap of *Memoirs*, Auberon Waugh, writing in *The Spectator*, said of *Christie Malry's Own Double Entry*: '. . . undoubtedly a masterpiece. If I had any say in the matter it would probably win the Nobel Prize for Literature.'

Auberon Waugh? *The Spectator*, bastion of the right-wing non-thinkers, opponents, one would assume, of any form of innovation? Odd. On the front flap of *Memoirs* there is a quote from the ubiquitous Anthony Burgess: '. . . the only living British author with the guts to reassess the novel form, extend its scope and still work in a recognisable fictional tradition'. So the reviews were not quite as persistently discouraging as BSJ would have you believe from his introduction to the same volume.

Consider then one Philip Pacey, writing in *Stand* in 1974,

the year after Johnson's death. Pacey's piece is respectful, earnest and predictable. Schoolmasterish. He argues, as any sensible person would, against Johnson's insistence that telling stories is telling lies. Then he describes his late friend as 'most especially a writer's writer . . . the joyousness and ingenuity of his craft is [sic] such that one can hardly read him and not be inspired to write . . .'

Or surely, to write better? To write without exposing the doubts about the process that every writer must to some extent experience, which, once exposed, only betray the reader's trust. The trust that one is telling a story, not telling lies nor recounting the lived reality. I refuse to say the truth. You can't call it that.

What I am trying to avoid saying is that for all the flashes of light that I find in B.S. Johnson's voice, for all that I like his ingenuous sharing of his doubts about his work, it doesn't really get him anywhere. Such experiments only undermine readers' expectations and hence their pleasure.

Moreover, I now realise that, for all his pretensions to originality, B.S. Johnson was derivative to a degree that is hard to take—Laurence Sterne and Flann O'Brien spring immediately to mind. What is unforgivable I suppose is that they were funnier. Innovation in writing does not come from cutting holes in the pages, monkeying about with the typography or publishing loose-leaf. It does not come from revealing the author's secret reservations with his project. It comes from writing better, writing more strongly.

B.S. Johnson did not understand what writing is about. He was confusing fiction with self-expression. That bit about nothing being an answer to the loneliness to the lack of loving is the give-away. It is Aristotle versus Plato all over again. He did not understand the essential nature of fiction, its strangeness, the way it has a life of its own which has nothing to do with the writer's life.

'. . . how can you convey truth in a vehicle of fiction? The two terms, *truth* and *fiction,* are opposites, and it must logically

be impossible.'
    Bullshit, BSJ.

Here is an anecdote another writer told me about B.S. Johnson, not a lie, not a story but a truth. See how far it gets you.

They met in Portland House, where they had both been involved in a programme for the BBC World Service, and they walked together down miles of corridors and out of the building to the pub. As they walked, Johnson kept his eyes on the ground and every so often he would bend down and pick up a paperclip. He could spot a paperclip from yards away, indoors or out. Never was there an eye for spotting lost paperclips like the eye of B.S. Johnson.

ALANNAH HOPKIN lives in Kinsale, Co Cork. She grew up in London and studied at Queen Mary University of London and the University of Essex. She has published two novels (Hamish Hamilton); her non-fiction books include *West Cork, the People & the Place* (The Collins Press, Cork). She has written guides to Ireland for Fodor's, Insight and Berlitz, and also writes about travel and visual art. She has reviewed literary fiction and biography since 1980 for many publications, including the *London Evening Standard*, the *Financial Times*, the *Irish Times* and the *Irish Examiner*. She has led writing workshops on the short story to M.A. level.

'You Can't Call it That' was published in The Cork Review (January 1999) and in *The London Magazine* (October 2000).

'Ripe' was first published in *London Tales* (Hamish Hamilton 1983).

'Coo' was broadcast on Campus Radio, University College Cork in January 1997.

'The Dogs of Inishere' was published in *Books Ireland* (July 1996) and *The Literary Review – New Irish Poetry and Prose* (Fairleigh Dickinson University, Madison, New Jersey, Summer 1997).

MICHAL AJVAZ, *The Golden Age.*
The Other City.

PIERRE ALBERT-BIROT, *Grabinoulor.*

YUZ ALESHKOVSKY, *Kangaroo.*

FELIPE ALFAU, *Chromos.*
Locos.

JOE AMATO, *Samuel Taylor's Last Night.*

IVAN ÂNGELO, *The Celebration.*
The Tower of Glass.

ANTÓNIO LOBO ANTUNES, *Knowledge of Hell.*
The Splendor of Portugal.

ALAIN ARIAS-MISSON, *Theatre of Incest.*

JOHN ASHBERY & JAMES SCHUYLER, *A Nest of Ninnies.*

ROBERT ASHLEY, *Perfect Lives.*

GABRIELA AVIGUR-ROTEM, *Heatwave and Crazy Birds.*

DJUNA BARNES, *Ladies Almanack.*
Ryder.

JOHN BARTH, *Letters.*
Sabbatical.

DONALD BARTHELME, *The King.*
Paradise.

SVETISLAV BASARA, *Chinese Letter.*

MIQUEL BAUÇÀ, *The Siege in the Room.*

RENÉ BELLETTO, *Dying.*

MAREK BIEŃCZYK, *Transparency.*

ANDREI BITOV, *Pushkin House.*

ANDREJ BLATNIK, *You Do Understand.*
Law of Desire.

LOUIS PAUL BOON, *Chapel Road.*
My Little War.
Summer in Termuren.

ROGER BOYLAN, *Killoyle.*

IGNÁCIO DE LOYOLA BRANDÃO,
Anonymous Celebrity.
Zero.

BONNIE BREMSER, *Troia: Mexican Memoirs.*

CHRISTINE BROOKE-ROSE,
Amalgamemnon.

BRIGID BROPHY, *In Transit.*
The Prancing Novelist.

GERALD L. BRUNS,
Modern Poetry and the Idea of Language.

GABRIELLE BURTON, *Heartbreak Hotel.*

MICHEL BUTOR, *Degrees.*
Mobile.

G. CABRERA INFANTE, *Infante's Inferno.*
Three Trapped Tigers.

JULIETA CAMPOS, *The Fear of Losing Eurydice.*

ANNE CARSON, *Eros the Bittersweet.*

ORLY CASTEL-BLOOM, *Dolly City.*

LOUIS-FERDINAND CÉLINE, *North.*
Conversations with Professor Y.
London Bridge.

MARIE CHAIX, *The Laurels of Lake Constance.*

HUGO CHARTERIS, *The Tide Is Right.*

ERIC CHEVILLARD, *Demolishing Nisard.*
The Author and Me.

MARC CHOLODENKO, *Mordechai Schamz.*

JOSHUA COHEN, *Witz.*

EMILY HOLMES COLEMAN, *The Shutter of Snow.*

ERIC CHEVILLARD, *The Author and Me.*

ROBERT COOVER, *A Night at the Movies.*

STANLEY CRAWFORD, *Log of the S.S. The Mrs Unguentine.*
Some Instructions to My Wife.

RENÉ CREVEL, *Putting My Foot in It.*

RALPH CUSACK, *Cadenza.*

NICHOLAS DELBANCO, *Sherbrookes.*
The Count of Concord.

NIGEL DENNIS, *Cards of Identity.*

PETER DIMOCK, *A Short Rhetoric for Leaving the Family.*

ARIEL DORFMAN, *Konfidenz.*

COLEMAN DOWELL, *Island People.*
Too Much Flesh and Jabez.

ARKADII DRAGOMOSHCHENKO,
Dust.

RIKKI DUCORNET, *Phosphor in Dreamland.*
The Complete Butcher's Tales.

RIKKI DUCORNET (cont.), *The Jade Cabinet.*
The Fountains of Neptune.

WILLIAM EASTLAKE, *The Bamboo Bed.*
Castle Keep.
Lyric of the Circle Heart.

JEAN ECHENOZ, *Chopin's Move.*

STANLEY ELKIN, *A Bad Man.*
Criers and Kibitzers, Kibitzers and Criers.
The Dick Gibson Show.
The Franchiser.
The Living End.
Mrs. Ted Bliss.

FRANÇOIS EMMANUEL, *Invitation to a Voyage.*

PAUL EMOND, *The Dance of a Sham.*

SALVADOR ESPRIU, *Ariadne in the Grotesque Labyrinth.*

LESLIE A. FIEDLER, *Love and Death in the American Novel.*

JUAN FILLOY, *Op Oloop.*

ANDY FITCH, *Pop Poetics.*

GUSTAVE FLAUBERT, *Bouvard and Pécuchet.*

KASS FLEISHER, *Talking out of School.*

JON FOSSE, *Aliss at the Fire.*
Melancholy.

FORD MADOX FORD, *The March of Literature.*

MAX FRISCH, *I'm Not Stiller.*
Man in the Holocene.

CARLOS FUENTES, *Christopher Unborn.*
Distant Relations.
Terra Nostra.
Where the Air Is Clear.

TAKEHIKO FUKUNAGA, *Flowers of Grass.*

WILLIAM GADDIS, JR., *The Recognitions.*

JANICE GALLOWAY, *Foreign Parts.*
The Trick Is to Keep Breathing.

WILLIAM H. GASS, *Life Sentences.*
The Tunnel.
The World Within the Word.
Willie Masters' Lonesome Wife.

GÉRARD GAVARRY, *Hoppla! 1 2 3.*

ETIENNE GILSON, *The Arts of the Beautiful.*
Forms and Substances in the Arts.

C. S. GISCOMBE, *Giscome Road.*
Here.

DOUGLAS GLOVER, *Bad News of the Heart.*

WITOLD GOMBROWICZ, *A Kind of Testament.*

PAULO EMÍLIO SALES GOMES, *P's Three Women.*

GEORGI GOSPODINOV, *Natural Novel.*

JUAN GOYTISOLO, *Count Julian.*
Juan the Landless.
Makbara.
Marks of Identity.

HENRY GREEN, *Blindness.*
Concluding.
Doting.
Nothing.

JACK GREEN, *Fire the Bastards!*

JIŘÍ GRUŠA, *The Questionnaire.*

MELA HARTWIG, *Am I a Redundant Human Being?*

JOHN HAWKES, *The Passion Artist.*
Whistlejacket.

ELIZABETH HEIGHWAY, ED., *Contemporary Georgian Fiction.*

AIDAN HIGGINS, *Balcony of Europe.*
Blind Man's Bluff.
Bornholm Night-Ferry.
Langrishe, Go Down.
Scenes from a Receding Past.

KEIZO HINO, *Isle of Dreams.*

KAZUSHI HOSAKA, *Plainsong.*

ALDOUS HUXLEY, *Antic Hay.*
Point Counter Point.
Those Barren Leaves.
Time Must Have a Stop.

NAOYUKI II, *The Shadow of a Blue Cat.*

DRAGO JANČAR, *The Tree with No Name.*

MIKHEIL JAVAKHISHVILI, *Kvachi.*

GERT JONKE, *The Distant Sound.*
Homage to Czerny.
The System of Vienna.

JACQUES JOUET, *Mountain R.*
Savage.
Upstaged.
MIEKO KANAI, *The Word Book.*
YORAM KANIUK, *Life on Sandpaper.*
ZURAB KARUMIDZE, *Dagny.*
JOHN KELLY, *From Out of the City.*
HUGH KENNER, *Flaubert, Joyce and Beckett: The Stoic Comedians.*
Joyce's Voices.
DANILO KIŠ, *The Attic.*
The Lute and the Scars.
Psalm 44.
A Tomb for Boris Davidovich.
ANITA KONKKA, *A Fool's Paradise.*
GEORGE KONRÁD, *The City Builder.*
TADEUSZ KONWICKI, *A Minor Apocalypse.*
The Polish Complex.
ANNA KORDZAIA-SAMADASHVILI, *Me, Margarita.*
MENIS KOUMANDAREAS, *Koula.*
ELAINE KRAF, *The Princess of 72nd Street.*
JIM KRUSOE, *Iceland.*
AYSE KULIN, *Farewell: A Mansion in Occupied Istanbul.*
EMILIO LASCANO TEGUI, *On Elegance While Sleeping.*
ERIC LAURRENT, *Do Not Touch.*
VIOLETTE LEDUC, *La Bâtarde.*
EDOUARD LEVÉ, *Autoportrait.*
Newspaper.
Suicide.
Works.
MARIO LEVI, *Istanbul Was a Fairy Tale.*
DEBORAH LEVY, *Billy and Girl.*
JOSÉ LEZAMA LIMA, *Paradiso.*
ROSA LIKSOM, *Dark Paradise.*
OSMAN LINS, *Avalovara.*
The Queen of the Prisons of Greece.
FLORIAN LIPUŠ, *The Errors of Young Tjaž.*
GORDON LISH, *Peru.*
ALF MACLOCHLAINN, *Out of Focus.*
Past Habitual.

The Corpus in the Library.
RON LOEWINSOHN, *Magnetic Field(s).*
YURI LOTMAN, *Non-Memoirs.*
D. KEITH MANO, *Take Five.*
MINA LOY, *Stories and Essays of Mina Loy.*
MICHELINE AHARONIAN MARCOM, *A Brief History of Yes.*
The Mirror in the Well.
BEN MARCUS, *The Age of Wire and String.*
WALLACE MARKFIELD, *Teitlebaum's Window.*
DAVID MARKSON, *Reader's Block.*
Wittgenstein's Mistress.
CAROLE MASO, *AVA.*
HISAKI MATSUURA, *Triangle.*
LADISLAV MATEJKA & KRYSTYNA POMORSKA, EDS., *Readings in Russian Poetics: Formalist & Structuralist Views.*
HARRY MATHEWS, *Cigarettes.*
The Conversions.
The Human Country.
The Journalist.
My Life in CIA.
Singular Pleasures.
The Sinking of the Odradek.
Stadium.
Tlooth.
HISAKI MATSUURA, *Triangle.*
DONAL MCLAUGHLIN, *beheading the virgin mary, and other stories.*
JOSEPH MCELROY, *Night Soul and Other Stories.*
ABDELWAHAB MEDDEB, *Talismano.*
GERHARD MEIER, *Isle of the Dead.*
HERMAN MELVILLE, *The Confidence-Man.*
AMANDA MICHALOPOULOU, *I'd Like.*
STEVEN MILLHAUSER, *The Barnum Museum.*
In the Penny Arcade.
RALPH J. MILLS, JR., *Essays on Poetry.*
MOMUS, *The Book of Jokes.*
CHRISTINE MONTALBETTI, *The Origin of Man.*
Western.

NICHOLAS MOSLEY, *Accident*.
Assassins.
Catastrophe Practice.
A Garden of Trees.
Hopeful Monsters.
Imago Bird.
Inventing God.
Look at the Dark.
Metamorphosis.
Natalie Natalia.
Serpent.

WARREN MOTTE, *Fables of the Novel: French Fiction since 1990*.
Fiction Now: The French Novel in the 21st Century.
Mirror Gazing.
Oulipo: A Primer of Potential Literature.

GERALD MURNANE, *Barley Patch*.
Inland.

YVES NAVARRE, *Our Share of Time*.
Sweet Tooth.

DOROTHY NELSON, *In Night's City*.
Tar and Feathers.

ESHKOL NEVO, *Homesick*.

WILFRIDO D. NOLLEDO, *But for the Lovers*.

BORIS A. NOVAK, *The Master of Insomnia*.

FLANN O'BRIEN, *At Swim-Two-Birds*.
The Best of Myles.
The Dalkey Archive.
The Hard Life.
The Poor Mouth.
The Third Policeman.

CLAUDE OLLIER, *The Mise-en-Scène*.
Wert and the Life Without End.

PATRIK OUŘEDNÍK, *Europeana*.
The Opportune Moment, 1855.

BORIS PAHOR, *Necropolis*.

FERNANDO DEL PASO, *News from the Empire*.
Palinuro of Mexico.

ROBERT PINGET, *The Inquisitory*.
Mahu or The Material.
Trio.

MANUEL PUIG, *Betrayed by Rita Hayworth*.

The Buenos Aires Affair.
Heartbreak Tango.

RAYMOND QUENEAU, *The Last Days*.
Odile.
Pierrot Mon Ami.
Saint Glinglin.

ANN QUIN, *Berg*.
Passages.
Three.
Tripticks.

ISHMAEL REED, *The Free-Lance Pallbearers*.
The Last Days of Louisiana Red.
Ishmael Reed: The Plays.
Juice!
The Terrible Threes.
The Terrible Twos.
Yellow Back Radio Broke-Down.

JASIA REICHARDT, *15 Journeys Warsaw to London*.

JOÃO UBALDO RIBEIRO, *House of the Fortunate Buddhas*.

JEAN RICARDOU, *Place Names*.

RAINER MARIA RILKE,
The Notebooks of Malte Laurids Brigge.

JULIÁN RÍOS, *The House of Ulysses*.
Larva: A Midsummer Night's Babel.
Poundemonium.

ALAIN ROBBE-GRILLET, *Project for a Revolution in New York*.
A Sentimental Novel.

AUGUSTO ROA BASTOS, *I the Supreme*.

DANIËL ROBBERECHTS, *Arriving in Avignon*.

JEAN ROLIN, *The Explosion of the Radiator Hose*.

OLIVIER ROLIN, *Hotel Crystal*.

ALIX CLEO ROUBAUD, *Alix's Journal*.

JACQUES ROUBAUD, *The Form of a City Changes Faster, Alas, Than the Human Heart*.
The Great Fire of London.
Hortense in Exile.
Hortense Is Abducted.
Mathematics: The Plurality of Worlds of Lewis.
Some Thing Black.

RAYMOND ROUSSEL, *Impressions of Africa.*

VEDRANA RUDAN, *Night.*

PABLO M. RUIZ, *Four Cold Chapters on the Possibility of Literature.*

GERMAN SADULAEV, *The Maya Pill.*

TOMAŽ ŠALAMUN, *Soy Realidad.*

LYDIE SALVAYRE, *The Company of Ghosts.*
The Lecture.
The Power of Flies.

LUIS RAFAEL SÁNCHEZ, *Macho Camacho's Beat.*

SEVERO SARDUY, *Cobra & Maitreya.*

NATHALIE SARRAUTE, *Do You Hear Them?*
Martereau.
The Planetarium.

STIG SÆTERBAKKEN, *Siamese.*
Self-Control.
Through the Night.

ARNO SCHMIDT, *Collected Novellas.*
Collected Stories.
Nobodaddy's Children.
Two Novels.

ASAF SCHURR, *Motti.*

GAIL SCOTT, *My Paris.*

DAMION SEARLS, *What We Were Doing and Where We Were Going.*

JUNE AKERS SEESE,
Is This What Other Women Feel Too?

BERNARD SHARE, *Inish.*
Transit.

VIKTOR SHKLOVSKY, *Bowstring.*
Literature and Cinematography.
Theory of Prose.
Third Factory.
Zoo, or Letters Not about Love.

PIERRE SINIAC, *The Collaborators.*

KJERSTI A. SKOMSVOLD,
The Faster I Walk, the Smaller I Am.

JOSEF ŠKVORECKÝ, *The Engineer of Human Souls.*

GILBERT SORRENTINO, *Aberration of Starlight.*
Blue Pastoral.
Crystal Vision.

Imaginative Qualities of Actual Things.
Mulligan Stew. Red the Fiend.
Steelwork.
Under the Shadow.

MARKO SOSIČ, *Ballerina, Ballerina.*

ANDRZEJ STASIUK, *Dukla.*
Fado.

GERTRUDE STEIN, *The Making of Americans.*
A Novel of Thank You.

LARS SVENDSEN, *A Philosophy of Evil.*

PIOTR SZEWC, *Annihilation.*

GONÇALO M. TAVARES, *A Man: Klaus Klump.*
Jerusalem.
Learning to Pray in the Age of Technique.

LUCIAN DAN TEODOROVICI,
Our Circus Presents…

NIKANOR TERATOLOGEN, *Assisted Living.*

STEFAN THEMERSON, *Hobson's Island.*
The Mystery of the Sardine.
Tom Harris.

TAEKO TOMIOKA, *Building Waves.*

JOHN TOOMEY, *Sleepwalker.*

DUMITRU TSEPENEAG, *Hotel Europa.*
The Necessary Marriage.
Pigeon Post.
Vain Art of the Fugue.

ESTHER TUSQUETS, *Stranded.*

DUBRAVKA UGRESIC, *Lend Me Your Character.*
Thank You for Not Reading.

TOR ULVEN, *Replacement.*

MATI UNT, *Brecht at Night.*
Diary of a Blood Donor.
Things in the Night.

ÁLVARO URIBE & OLIVIA SEARS, EDS.,
Best of Contemporary Mexican Fiction.

ELOY URROZ, *Friction.*
The Obstacles.

LUISA VALENZUELA, *Dark Desires and the Others.*
He Who Searches.

PAUL VERHAEGHEN, *Omega Minor.*

BORIS VIAN, *Heartsnatcher.*